THE POSSUM KING

J.R. Nunchucks

ISBN: 9798836635725

Imprint: Independently published

I would like to give a special thanks to me, for writing the best book you will ever read.

You're welcome.

Table of Contents

Chapter 1

Wincing from the light piercing through the dusty kitchen window, Gary makes his way over to start the pot of coffee he prepared the night before. He rubs his forehead and groans as he opens his fridge and picks up a carton of eggs and a small bloody slab of fresh meat. He turns on the stove and cracks a few eggs in his unkempt cast iron skillet, stained with residue and food from previous meals. Gary takes the cold meat and throws it into the skillet with the eggs, and lifelessly adds salt and pepper while still half asleep. He peers through the kitchen window and runs his hand through his long greasy black hair. As if lost in thought he stares out into his front yard looking upon a large field of tall grass. The rays from the sun bounce off the dew drops as vibrant colors sparkle across the field. The birds whistle and sing as if they were competing with the splendor of the sunrise. To most people this would be a scene worthy of a painting, worthy of remembering, breathtaking: but all Gary can see is the same day being forcefully replayed over and over in his head. A day that lingers in his mind and no matter how hard he tries he is unable to cast it out.

The coffee pot gurgles and hisses as if it's trying to catch its breath and Gary snaps out of his distant daze. He plates his food and pours a brimming cup of coffee and walks across the tattered tiled floor to his small round wooden kitchen table. Plopping down on his creaky fold out chair, the smell of his warm nutritious breakfast overtakes his senses. He inhales deeply and for a moment there is a sense of peace. That peaceful feeling is quickly snuffed out by the odor of Gary's unwashed wife beater and worn out boxer briefs. Exhaling with a big sigh he cuts into his egg with his fork. Egg yolk swims across his plate surrounding the small slab of meat.

After Gary finishes his eggs he begins cutting the meat. He grabs an old hunting knife already on the table and begins making his first slice keeping the meat steady with his rough fingers. As he rocks the sharp blade back and forth cutting deeper and deeper, his eyes turn tense and he grits his teeth. His breathing becomes heavy as if he's having some sort of allergic reaction but it's just pure rage. Gary's whole body shakes as he cuts and cuts until the meat is almost unrecognizable, shredded.

Pausing and trying to regain control Gary moves his hair out of his eyes and begins to calmly eat the rest of his breakfast. He sips his dark sludge-like coffee in between bites only to be interrupted from a painful bite as his teeth scrape against a tiny silver ball. Gary grimaces and spits out the buckshot and washes the metallic taste from his mouth with a swig of coffee. After his meal, Gary stands up with his dishes and sets them on the heaping pile of dirty plates and bowls already occupying the sink.

Even after a warm shower, a close shave, and half a cup of coffee, Gary was struggling to wake up. He pulls out his clothes from his dresser and throws them on his twin sized bed with the sheets and blankets strewn about. He takes notice of the turned over picture frame on the dresser and he feels sad for a moment. Knowing what the picture is of is enough for him. Seeing it again would be too painful.

Gary slips his tall slender frame into his naturally faded blue jeans and buttoning up his untucked tan short sleeved shirt, Gary was almost ready to start his day. He grabbed his compact pistol off his night stand and put it inside his waistband holster, hidden by his untucked shirt along with two extra loaded magazines. After making his way back through his awfully wallpapered hallway into his kitchen he grabs his hunting knife and kneels down to holster it around his ankle above his brown boot. He stands back up and takes his half empty coffee cup off the table. He then walks over to the counter and grabs his little black day planner, a pack of cigarettes, a cheap lighter, and his car keys which he keeps next to his yellow wall mounted phone with an unnaturally long curly cord.

He opens his creaky front door and is greeted by a rush of thick warm air. Stepping out onto the half rotten porch he closes the door behind him and sets his keys, planner, and coffee down on the wooden railing of the porch, freeing his hands for his morning cigarette. Gary guards his cigarette from the light breeze with his hand cupped as he flicks the lighter to life and takes his first drag of poison for the day. Taking in the scenery again, but this time without the window obscuring the view with its dusty coat, Gary lets his mind wander. His eyes scan the large field, watching the grass bend to the will of the gentle breeze. The songs of the birds draw his gaze to the various trees surrounding the house, trying to spot one of these hidden performers.

Finishing most of his morning cigarette, he tosses the butt into an old metal bucket by his feet. Grabbing his belongings off the railing, he makes his way to his old windowless white van parked in front of the house. The van is pretty old with rust filling in where paint is missing, which is most of the van at this point. Covered in dents and dust, one could barely make out the decals on the vehicle. *Gophers Get Got* is written on both sides of the van with a graphic of a cartoon gopher smiling behind a set of cross hairs and Gary's home phone number centered underneath. The soft steps of the porch bow slightly as he makes his way down. He fumbles with his keys and tries not to spill any coffee as he unlocks his van. He hops into the old rust bucket and throws his cigarettes and lighter onto the filthy, once black dashboard: a small dust plume arises from the dash. He puts the coffee carefully down in the torn up passenger seat because the coffee mug's handle does not allow for it to fit in the van's cup holders.

Gary leans over the steering wheel and turns the key.

"Come on come on," he murmurs over the engine's sad mechanical breaths.

The first few tries, the engine lets out a brief high pitched cry immediately followed by desperate grinding whimpers. Violently he strikes the steering wheel multiple times with the palm of his hand.

"Piece of mother….garbage trash van…idiot," he grunts loudly as he repositions himself over the steering wheel putting his whole body weight into turning the key. His teeth gritting and showing, his face distraught and angered, his hair dancing wildly as his head shakes uncontrollably he finally starts the van. Just as quickly as the anger overtook Gary, it vanished. Gary combs his fingers through his hair straightening out the wild strays from his little episode and picks up his day planner. He opens it up and begins flipping the crinkled pages slowly as he tracks down the right day.

"Mmhmm" he moaned quietly to himself and placed his finger on his first job of the day.

Mrs. Carsh, lots of gophers, was written in the block above her address. Gary lights another cigarette, buckles his seat belt, grabs his coffee and drives off down the long gravel driveway. A massive cloud of dust and thick exhaust follows closely behind.

As Gary drives down the rural roads, he passes by many old beautiful houses separated from each other by large fields of grass and trees. Gary's home is a few miles from town and he prefers to conduct his business in the countryside. He blinks his heavy eyes trying to wake himself up, and starts scanning through radio stations to have something audible to focus on. He balances the cigarette on his lips in order to change through the various radio stations while also holding on to his coffee cup. Irritated at his choices of stations, he shuts off the radio and shifts his focus back on the road just in time to see a deer carcass rapidly approaching. He jerks the steering wheel to the right with his left hand while still holding his coffee in the other, but it's too late. The front right wheel of the decrepit van pummels over the head of the sleeping doe carcass. The van seems to almost leap over it with a loud thud. Gary drops his cup and spills lukewarm coffee all over himself.His cigarette falls from his lips to the floorboard.

SCREEEEEEECH!

The van slides as he slams his boot against the brakes. His body is thrown back against the seat as the vehicle finally comes to a complete stop.

With a white knuckle grip on the steering wheel his breathing becomes intensified and filled with fury, his blue eyes grow wild as his face trembles. He puts the van in park and flings the keys out of the ignition. He reaches over to the passenger side and grabs the empty cup and swings open the driver side door and climbs out of the van. Fast walking with a slight hunch in his back and his arms stiff, he follows the curving skid marks back to the dead deer. He breathes in the smell of burnt rubber and looks over his shoulder at his van as he marches toward the deer, doing a quick survey of any new damage. He whips his head back around and continues glaring at the deer through the black strands of hair covering his face. In mid strut he hurls his coffee cup with a sidearm throw at the deer's head. The cup breaks against the asphalt in front of the deer and pieces of ceramic are launched at the lying animal. Gary stops in front of the lifeless carcass and towers over it. Then he draws his sidearm from its holster. He checks up and down the road to see if any cars are coming. Once confirming the coast is clear he begins firing rounds off in the roadkill. His face is distorted and menacing as he unloads an entire clip into the body.

The gunshots ring loudly to where Gary fails to hear the oncoming school bus that just turned a corner and is fast approaching in the other lane. The bus driver slows down and maneuvers to avoid hitting Gary's awkwardly parked van. The bus passes behind Gary, and the children aboard see a tall skinny forty some year old man pointing a smoking gun at a dead animal. They are horrified. Their screams capture Gary's attention and he slowly turns around. He gives a nod and a half smile trying to assure the kids with a look that everything is alright as he snaps the slide of his pistol close and reholsters it. The yellow bus passes the scene and begins to quickly pick up speed. The kids in the back of the bus have their hands and faces pressed up against the window pane with their eyes wide and their jaws gaping. Gary gives them a wave.

He walks back over to the deer and hovers over it. The morning sun casts a shadow of him onto the deer. He brushes back his hair with both of his slender hands and adjusts it behind his ears and crouches down. Leaning close to the deer's face he lifts up its soft, cold, stiff ear with his left hand and whispers, "If I see any of your woodland deer friends prancing around in my streets, I will see to it that their legs be removed."

He lifts his pant leg with his other arm and draws his hunting knife and points it at the deer. "And then I will release your legless friends back into the wild, where they will not be a driving hazard for me anymore."

He lets go of the ear and spits in the deer's face and sheaths the blade.

Standing to his feet Gary walks briskly towards the van and opens up the passenger door. He crawls half way in looking for his pack of smokes and his lighter which he eventually finds under the driver seat. He gets out and shuts the door, leaning against the outside of the van. He sparks up another stick and places the remaining pack and lighter in his front shirt pocket. Contemplating what just happened and thinking of how angry he became, he tilts his head back and breathes deeply through his nostrils and exhales slowly. He does this a few more times before taking another drag off of his cigarette and walks to the front of the van. He discovers that the right side of his silverish rust colored bumper is sagging to the ground. Frowning and angry again he marches to the rear of the van and opens the doors. In the oncoming lane, an expensive looking black luxury car slows down as it maneuvers around the van. As the car is passing, the windows roll down and a group of teenagers begin yelling profanities at Gary. They tell him to move his piece of crap van out of the way, paying no regard to if he is alright even though he has clearly been in an accident. Expressionless to the point of being creepy, Gary stares the highschoolers down in the shiny black car as it drives by.

He pulls himself up into the back of his vehicle looking for some tape which normally would be in his plastic bucket with an assortment of go-to tools and items. But a lot of the supplies were scattered about from the incident. After a minute or so of digging around, he finds the roll of tape he was looking for and goes over to start patching up his bumper.

He manages to get the bumper off the ground using the tape. Taking a step back and crossing his arms he inspects his work and flicks his cigarette onto the ground. If his van wasn't pitiful enough looking before, it sure was now. He climbs back in the driver side of the car and tosses the tape on the floor of the passenger side and hears his keys jingle under the impact. He reaches down to grab them and as he sits back up, he sees the still lying deer in the passenger side mirror. His lips tighten and he looks out ahead over the hood of his car, then behind him through the driver side mirror. His glances bounce back and forth a few times checking for any traffic, deciding if he should give into the unnaturally strong impulse he is feeling. Sighing, he goes back outside and opens the back doors of the van pulling out an empty red gas can and a piece of a green garden hose.

He checks the road one more time for any approaching vehicles, then opens the van's gas tank and puts the green piece of hose down in it. Gary kneels down and opens the red gas can and then proceeds to suck on the hose. Eventually gas floods into Gary's mouth and he quickly spits it out to the side hacking and coughing, dribbling gasoline on his shirt. Before too much gas spills onto the street, he quickly puts the red gas can underneath the hose. At about half full, Gary pulls the hose out and closes the vehicle's gas tank. The fumes make Gary a little light headed as he stands up with the can of gas. He shakes it off and follows the black skid marks back to the doe.

Once again he looms over this dead animal. This time drenching it in gasoline. From the head to the tail he sloshes the can back and forth making sure every part of the deer is soaked. He tosses the empty can back toward the vehicle. Gary stares blankly into the deers lifeless eyes as he pulls out his lighter and pack of smokes from his breast pocket. He pulls one of his last cigarettes slowly and carefully with his teeth. Calmly, he places the pack back in his pocket while holding on to the lighter and staring at the deer. Guarding the cigarette from the wind with his hand he lights it, refusing to break eye contact with the animal. Once lit, he holds the cheap lighter above his shirt pocket and pauses for a few seconds, then drops it in with the pack of remaining cigarettes, trying to build more suspense as if the deer is conscious and watching him. He takes one long deep inhale, his cheeks collapse. Then he lets out a long controlled exhale of smoke out of the corner of his mouth. Gary bends over and rests a hand on his knee and holds up the cigarette. He gives it a solid flick, launching the cigarette in an arch it spins as it descends. It lands right on top of the deer and a wave of heat and fire spread over the carcass.

Chapter 2

Outside in her front yard, Mrs. Carsh waters her many plants and colorful flowers with her green watering can. She loves gardening and has the best lawn and flower beds in the area. The grass in the front yard is nearly perfect. No weeds, no thinning areas, just thick luscious green cut grass. The flower bed which is separated from the lawn by tastefully placed stones is a beautiful arrangement of wild bright colors which contrasts well against the backdrop of the white country home. She recognizes the sputtering engine of Gary's old van as he usually drives by her house to and from various jobs a few times a week. Except this time Gary wasn't passing by, but turned on to the dirt road leading to her home. The beautiful landscape of her property is tarnished from the pollutants spewing from the van as it makes its way into a gravel lot big enough for five or six vehicles. The engine winds down to a quiet ticking and Gary hops out of the van to greet his customer.

"Good morning Mrs. Carsh," Gary says as he walks up to shake her hand.

She puts down her watering can and makes her way toward Gary. "Good morning Mr. Bilson."

"Just Gary." He puts out his hand.

She smiles and shakes his hand. "It's been a while." Instantly smelling the strong scent of gasoline fumes permeating from his shirt she asks, "Why do you smell like gasoline at nine in the morning?"

He scratches the back of his head and looks down at the ground. "Had some car trouble this morning ma'am."

She leans to one side and parts her long blond hair from her shades looking around Gary to examine the car. Her eyebrows ascend above her bug eyed sunglasses. "Ya, it looks like it" she says with a snarky tone wondering to herself if she should have hired someone else for the job. "Well come on back around and I'll show you what needs to be taken care of."

The backyard was even more of a sight to behold than the front yard. To the back of the property at the edge of the lawn is a tree line, with an array of various ferns and trees descending down a slope to a river bank. Small white caps round the tops of the current as the clear water flows over the stoney floor of the river. The property is encompassed by a wooden white fence with more colorful flowers lining the edges of the back yard. The only eye sore of this manicured paradise were the mounds of dirt scattered about the lawn.

"Right there." Mrs Carsh points to the dirt mounds. "All this hard work I do only to be undone by varmints." She sighs.

"Doesn't look like there's too many, maybe five or six. Josh couldn't take care of this for you?" Gary said curiously.

"My husband is on some fancy corporate retreat. Even if he was home he would probably just feed em and try to house train em. He's kinda a softy when it comes to critters. I can deal with bugs and slugs but I don't like dealing with these mole things or whatever they are. I'll let you get to it. Just dont hurt them now. I'll be in the front working in the yard." Mrs. Karch said with a mild sense of concern in her tone.

Gary circles the mounds of dirt like a warden. His arms are crossed and his eyes narrow. He kneels down over the top of a mound and gently brushes the dirt away and starts feeling around with his hand. After a few moments a tiny tunnel is exposed. Going prone with his nose inches from the hole Gary whispers, "It's nothing personal, but the lady would rather have pretty blades of grass than a living creature dwelling in her space...sorry guys. I'll give you about ten minutes to clear out and then it's gonna get ugly. Again, sorry about this."

He stands back up and makes his way back to the van. Mrs. Carsh is pulling weeds out of the front bed with her knee pads on under the shade of her enormous sun hat. The back doors of the van creak open and Gary looks at the mess of tools and supplies lying all over the floor from the accident. Shaking his head and sighing he hoists himself in the van and picks up a giant spool of black rubber hose. He looks at the empty gas can on his way out and for a short moment wonders if he can use that instead of his regular gopher trapping techniques. Gary sticks with the hose and returns to the back yard with his spool.

A big prickly bush fights with Gary as he screws one end of the hose to the spigot on the back side of the house. He unravels the hose by kicking the spool. After a few kicks it rolls down the lawn and falls near the dirt mounds and he begins unraveling the rest of the hose. Once he is finished he sticks the hose into one of the holes.

Mrs. Carsh makes her way to the back yard. "You want some lemonade? I'm about to make a fresh batch, gett'n hot out here."

Gary gives a thumbs up and smiles. He returns to the van to get a few more items needed for the job;a white plastic bucket and a twenty gauge shotgun that is always kept loaded hanging on the wall of the van. With the gun and the bucket in one hand he turns the hose on with the other and water begins flooding the hole. He struts back to the mound and places the bucket upside down a few feet from the hole and sits down with the gun in his lap and waits. By the time Gary lights another cigarette from his shirt pocket, water starts to overflow out of the hole. Two gophers also make an appearance trying to escape from drowning. The gophers are soaked and confused. Blinded by the blazing sun as they emerge from their dark dwelling place, they are frozen stiff in fear. Gary leans over with his elbow on his knee and takes aim at the first gopher, the barrel almost touching it. Mrs. Carsh opens the sliding door and steps out onto the back porch only to drop Gary's fresh squeezed lemonade at the sound of a shotgun blast. Mrs. Carsh's scream is quickly drowned out by another blast from Gary's firearm. He stands up and moves the hose to another hole.

"What is wrong with you! I said don't hurt them!" She screams as she stands in a puddle of fresh lemonade.

"With all due respect ma'am, they prolly didn't feel a thing." Gary said, pumping his shotgun ready to take on more gophers.

"Is this standard practice for pest control?" Her voice was shaky with exasperation.

"It saves on costs which means I save you money." He said, amused at her reaction to his methods.

Mrs. Carsh was dumbfounded. She just couldn't believe this is how a pest control business could operate. She went back inside and slammed the sliding door behind her.

By the time Gary was done he had slayed seven gophers. He rolled the hose back up and returned it and the shotgun to the van. Every bloodied gopher and its scattered pieces were picked up and thrown into the bucket and put away. When he closed the van door, Mrs. Carsh was standing there giving Gary the stink eye. She ripped a check out of her checkbook and handed it to him without saying a word, but her face said enough. Even under those big sunglasses Gary could tell she was not impressed.

"Thank you ma'am, tell Josh I said hi," Gary said smiling, trying to remain professional.

She turned around and made for the front door.

As Gary opens the driver side door he yells out. "Oh Mrs. Carsh, if you would like, for a small fee I can sew the gophers skins together to make a lap blanket, or a little scarf, or a coin purse."

She didn't even turn around. She just kept walking, shaking her head, and went inside her home.

Back in his dusty van he grabs his day planner and flips through the sun bleached pages putting his finger on the next job for the day. Familiar with the property he knows exactly how to get there. It's back on the same road as his home just a few lots down. Battling the ignition once again, Gary is muttering and swearing under his breath as he finally succeeds in getting the engine started. The van makes a wide u-turn as it back tracks down the driveway. He stops at the end of the driveway and checks for traffic before turning onto the main road. The Carsh's mailbox is less than an arm's reach next to Gary. He opens the mailbox to see if the Carsh's had checked their mail from yesterday. The mailbox had about two days worth of mail in it. He reaches and twists out the window and with both hands grabs all the mail and throws it on the passenger seat. "That'll teach you to not yell at me. Don't hurt the gophers Gary!" He said childishly, scrunching his nose and making a face. "Take care of the mole things, just don't hurt them Mr. Bilson, they have feelings and need love Mr. Bilson, my sunglasses make my face look like an insect Gary Bilson." He continued to mock Mrs. Carsh as he drove back down the road towards the next job site.

Knock Knock Knock. Gary pounds his fist on the white door. As he waits for an answer he swivels his head around surveying the property. It's not as well maintained as the last house but then again no one's property could live up to the Carsh's standards of perfection. The lawn was in desperate need of mowing and there were only bushes and shrubs surrounding the house, no flowers to be seen. A basketball hoop stood in the driveway and a couple of bikes lay in the grass next to it. Gary noticed they didn't have a garage, just a wide driveway with only his van parked in it. He raises his hand to knock once more and as he motions to hit the door it swings open and a teenage boy is standing there looking up at him.

"Are your parents home?" Gary said.

"No." The boy replied.

"Shouldn't you be in school?" He said with a confused look on his face.

"No, my mom says the last day of school is a waste of time and I should just stay home and wait for the exterminator." He starts to shut the door.

Gary pushes back on the door.

"I am the exterminator, and how am I getting paid if your parents arent home?" He said sternly with a subtle scowl.

"She left some money in an envelope. You can have it when you finish." The kid gently closes the door.

Gary flops his arms and sighs. Irritated, he starts gathering his supplies from his van and starts setting up in the backyard. He takes the big spool of hose and makes his way through the side gate leading to a big fenced-in backyard. The yard is a little overgrown, making it more difficult to find the gopher holes at a glance but he manages. Once found, Gary brings the shotgun and the bucket around. He notices two kids staring at him and his firearm from the kitchen window. Immediately the kids swing open the back door and rush towards Gary.

The younger kid excitedly asks, "Are you gonna blast the gophers?!" He pretends to hold a gun towards the general direction of the mounds of dirt and starts making loud machine gun noises with his high pitched voice.

"You know a better way?" Gary replied, annoyed at the stupid question. But at the same time flattered that someone took interest in his method.

The older kid chimed in, "Can we watch?"

"Sure, now unroll this hose and hook it up to the spigot."

The two brothers roll the spool towards the house as Gary searches for a good spot to place his bucket and reload his shotgun. He grabs a box of shells out of the bucket, then flips the bucket to sit on it. With his gun in his lap he starts loading shells, each click of the shell being chambered causes excitement and chatter between the two brothers.

"Ok we hooked it up!" The younger kid yelled to Gary.

Gary motioned them to come. They started sprinting towards him.

"Well bring the other end of the hose here dummies."

Too excited and too young to really be offended by Gary's demeanor, they run back giddily to get the spool. They unravel the hose and are ready to watch the exterminator exterminate these vermin with excessive force. Still sitting on the bucket Gary reaches into his pocket. Gary grabs one of his last remaining cigarettes and flicks his lighter on.

"You're gonna die." The young kid said to him, wiping his dirty hands on his camo shorts.

"Excuse me?" He replied with one raised eyebrow, turning off the lighter and tossing it in his shirt pocket.

"You're smoking, you're gonna die." He said sternly and authoritatively to Gary.

He locks eyes with the kid and takes one long slow drag, then blows smoke out of the corner of his mouth. With the cigarette between his two fingers he lowers it down to the kids face. The older brother is just watching curiously at the interaction.

"What's your name kid?"

"Kyle." He said, crossing his arms in defiance of Gary's actions.

"Well Kyle, don't knock it till you try it." Swirling the cigarette in an enticing figure eight motion in front of his face.

"I don't want that one, your mouth has been on it. I'll try a new one." Kyle said in his prepubescent high pitched voice.

"Kyle, that's not a good idea." The older brother said with a shake in his voice. Watching this unfold has made him concerned, nervous and uncomfortable.

"Don't tell me what to do Cody."

Gary glanced at Cody and gave him a grim smile. He hands Kyle the pack of remaining cigarettes. Kyle takes them with his eyes wide and full of discovery and begins to take one out. When the cigarette is half way out of the box, Kyle looks Gary straight in the eyes. Deadpan, he opens his hands in a theatrical manner as if performing a magic trick and drops the pack. Then stomps and smothers the pack of smokes.

"Ta Dah! You're welcome. I just saved your life." Kyle said proudly.

A wave of emotions swept over Gary as he stared angrily at the kid. At first he was enraged, but Gary had a way of controlling his anger around other people. He then felt a strange feeling he hadn't felt in a long time. The feeling that someone, in a small way, cared about him. He began thinking back to when he felt this before, getting lost in his past for a brief moment. His eyes snapped back to the present and being deeply touched he cleared his throat. "Who wants to massacre some gophers?"

The mood in the air instantly transformed back to excitement as Kyle leaps up in the air with his hand raised high. "I DO! I DO!".

"Brody, go turn the hose on. Kyle, stick the hose next to the hole so the water pours into it."

"My name is Cody!" The older brother yelled back at Gary as he ran to turn the hose on.

Kyle, overflowing with joy, took the hose and knelt down next to a mound and carefully positioned the hose over top of the hole. He stood back up dusting off his knees with a smile on his face. Gary stood up from the bucket holding his shotgun with one hand and pointing to the bucket with the other, signaling Kyle to take his place. The water starts flowing into the dirt and Cody runs back to join the hunt. Kyle sits on the bucket and stairs at the water flowing into the hole, waiting with anticipation to see what will happen next. His view is suddenly obscured by steel and wood as Gary holds the shotgun in front of his face. Cody is once again uncomfortable.

"Me?" He said, looking up and confused at the tall and lanky exterminator.

Gary gives him a nod of approval. "You're old enough. And if you haven't learned to shoot yet, your parents are doing you a disservice."

His now sweaty palms grab the gun and he fumbles to figure out how to hold it correctly. Gary gives him a loud aggressive snap of the fingers. "Hey!" He barks at Kyle, and the kid freezes in place hoping for some help. "Keep your slimy hands away from the trigger until you're ready to shoot." Gary moves to stand behind him and grabs the shotgun and gently brings it to his shoulder. He steps to Kyle's side and pretends to hold a shotgun, showing Kyle what to do next. "Put your cheek up to the stock like this. Now click that safety off and keep your finger off the trigger until you see a gopher. Then, slowly put your finger on the trigger. Take your time and aim, and do your country proud by knowing how to properly operate this fine gopher killing contraption."

Completely focused and with a sense of encouragement, Kyle waits; holding the firearm up to his shoulder. Gary habitually goes to grab another cigarette then rolls his eyes remembering they were just destroyed. Everyone is quiet, only the sound of the flowing water can be heard and the occasional car passing in the distance. Cody looks at his brother and is scared that something will go wrong. Then he looks at Gary trying to find a source of comfort that everything will be alright. The exterminator puts his hands over his ears, then looks at Cody. Cody mimics Gary and goes back to staring down the flooding hole, his heart pounding in his ears.

The first gopher breaks the surface, soaked and rattled. It stops moving and becomes paraylyzed in place. Kyle's eyes light up and his body tenses as he stares down the steel barrel at the rodent. Gary looks at Kyle, then at the gopher, then back at kyle. "You gonna shoot it?" He asks impatiently. Three more gophers spring out of the hole and are stunned still. Kyle begins to fidget his shoulders trying to get comfortable behind the gun. The gophers start to come to and begin to scurry. With one quick motion Gary swiftly clutches the shotgun out of Kyle's hands and brings it to a firing position. "Cover your ears!" Gary yells in frustration, and immediately starts blasting away at the gophers. Each shot was followed by a pump of the shotgun and a swinging of the barrel from gopher to gopher like a focused laser. Kyle and Cody were mesmerized by Gary's skill and speed. In seconds the action was done and there in the grass lay four fresh carcasess.

"Throw 'em in the bucket and move the hose to the next hole." Gary ordered as he trudged over to the next kill zone. The kids moved quickly and efficiently, something about a guy with a gun has a way of motivating. After a few rotations of flood, shoot, collect, reload, they were developing a synergy together.

"I think we got 'em all." Gary said approvingly. "Time to pack it in."

Cody rolled the hose up and Kyle took the bucket of dead animals to the van. Gary climbed into the van, reloaded and racked the shotgun, then motioned for Kyle to hand him the bucket. He couldn't help but notice that Kyle seemed a bit down compared to how he acted when they first started working.

"What's your deal kid, you fall in love with the gophers?" He asked with a chuckle.

"Next time." Kyle said and looked at Gary with a determined spirit. "I can do it."

Gary nodded as he put the bucket in the corner of the van stacking random supplies around it so it wouldn't tip over as he drove. Brushing his hands together he smiles and says, "I'll believe it when I see it."

He hops out of the van and slams the door only to reveal Cody with an outstretched arm holding an envelope. "Here you go Mr...uh."

"Bilson." Gary replied as he took the clean crisp envelope with his blood stained fingers. He opened it up and took out the cash to count it. He mumbles numbers under his breath as he fans through the bills. "This isn't enough. You're short." He said wincing at Cody as if he is the one to blame. Cody just shrugs his shoulders and trots off. Gary rolls his eyes and climbs into the driver seat and closes the door. Kyle follows him and stares at him from the other side of the window. The window squeaks as it makes its way down. "What are you staring at, kid?"

"I had fun today sir. I wish there were more gophers to murder." Kyle told him, drooping his head and kicking around the dirt.

"You have any pets? Cat, dog, hamster…?" Gary said to the mopey kid.

"I have a pet rabbit." Kyle said, a small smile cracks from the corners of his mouth.

"Well, if you need that dead, give me a call and we can have some more fun killin."

Kyle's smile left him.

Chapter 3

With all the appointments for the day completed, his stomach rumbles as he makes his way into town for some lunch. His mind kept replaying the events of the morning over and over, thinking about how fun it was to have some help from Cody and Kyle. He felt like a mentor, a dad, somebody that someone looked up to even if it was for only a moment. He couldn't stop thinking about it. The tiny voice of Kyle saying "I had fun today sir" played repeatedly in his head, trying to remember the last time he had done anything that resembled fun. These thoughts paired with the fresh air rushing in through the window as he drives makes for a good morning for Gary. He might even be happy.

Off the main road in town is Gary's go to lunch spot; an independently owned convenience store. He pulls into the parking lot of *Margret's Mart*, right next to an expensive looking black luxury car. He throws the van in park and sticks his neck out of the window looking at the car and then inside the mart. He sees a group of highschool kids horseplaying. The same kids that rudely passed him by earlier this morning. The brief feeling of happiness was drowned out by a quiet flood of bitterness and fury. He rips the keys out of the ignition and gets out of his vehicle and walks around to the black car. Hot and sunny outside, the car has all the windows down. Gary checks his surroundings, making sure no one notices him. He reaches into the driver side window and pops open the trunk. With haste he walks around the back of the car looking over his shoulder in paranoia. He approaches his van and swings open the doors. He steps in, tip toes and meunevers around the various tools and supplies on the floor and grabs the bucket in the corner and makes his way back out. He puts his head down and keeps his eyes up towards the convenience store as he lifts the fancy car's trunk up and dumps all the dead gophers and pieces of gophers in. Trying to be as silent as possible he gently closes the trunk and throws his bucket in the back of his vehicle and makes his way inside the mart.

The little bell above the door rings as he enters and is immediately greeted by the owner.

"Hey Gary! Just in time, just put the hot dogs on." Her soothing voice caused the anger in Gary to subside a bit.

"Lucky me." He smiled back. Taking the time during this quick interaction to admire the owner's long wavy red hair and bright blue cyes. His smile refused to leave as he walked to the back of the store to grab his hot lunch from under the heat lamp. He grabs a hot dog and a bun and tops it with all the fixings he can. Relish, ketchup, mayo, mustard, onions, jalapenos, and even nacho cheese make its way on this monstrosity of a hotdog. Somehow he is able to close the container around the hotdog, keeping all the toppings inside. Gary makes his way to the other side of the store to grab his cold beverage. He avoids the obnoxious highschool kids playing hooky on their last day of school and overhears them trying to get an older gentleman to buy them beer. He grips a cold tall can of cheap beer and heads to the front counter.

"One hotdog, one tallboy and....." She says and starts to reach behind her grabbing Gary's pack of choice cigarettes off the display.

"Oh not today Margret." Gary waved away the pack of smokes and shook his head.

"You're quitting? I'm impressed." She said with a genuine smile nodding her head in approval.

His eyes are drawn to a big glass jar filled with a colorful array of lollipops. He grabs a big handful and drops them on the counter. "I might need these though." He was unsure about this decision and that his new lifestyle change might be harder than he thought. But what Kyle said to him made an impact.

Margret grabbed a plastic bag and whipped it open and shoveled the lollipops in. "Good idea."

They smiled at each other and Gary paid for his goods and grabbed his items. The other older gentleman shopping got behind Gary and placed his snacks on the counter.

"Excuse me Miss, those kids are trying to get somebody to buy beer for them. I just thought you should know."

Margret shouts loudly at the group, "Get out of my store!"

The kids start laughing and hurling insults at Margret as they leave the store. Gary stares them down with hellish eyes as they stand around their car pulling out vape pens from their letterman jackets. Margret sees how angry Gary's face seems to be and she gently taps his shoulder. "It's fine. I get people like that coming in all the time."

Gary zones out still looking out the store window, insidious thoughts of revenge fill his mind. "See you Monday." He whispered, choked up in his own anger as he exited the mart.

Passing through a strongly strawberry scented vape cloud, Gary waves his free hand in front of him trying to clear the air as he opens the van. With a look of disgust he gets in the van and rolls the window down just a crack to listen to the highschool kids conversation. He overhears them laughing and using young people's slang that he found difficult to decipher, but he did manage to pick up that they were having a party at what seemed to be the leader of this little pack's house. He was a big guy with a short buzz cut, big jaw line but had a stupid face.

They were scheming on how to get beer for the party but decided to head back to Stupid Face's house for some lunch and gaming. The twisted gears in Gary's head clicked and he waited patiently for them to lead the way.

A few minutes go by of eye-roll inducing bro laughter before the pack finally hops into daddy's fancy car and begins to head home. Gary watches as they pull out of the parking lot and head down the main road. He follows them, keeping a good distance behind them just close enough to track them. They turn down a side street and make their way into a ritzy neighborhood with large expensive homes and cars. Each lawn looked as if it were cut today, freshly painted fences, even the garages that had the doors open were organized and tidy inside. Gary noticed the black car turning onto a street with a sign reading *Dead End*, so instead of following, he watched from afar and saw the car turn into the driveway of a two story white house with gray trim.He pulls over, while keeping the van running he gets out and walks down the cul de sac. The pack of bros head inside and Gary stands before the oversized house.

Normally, he would be content with just leaving some gophers in the trunk of their car. But after the incident at the convenience store, he didn't see a punishment that fit the unforgivable crime of insulting Margret so he needed to get creative. He stood there with his arms crossed and breaking pose only to unwrap a lollipop from his pocket, glaring at the home as he sucked on his candy. Silhouettes of the bro pack appear in the second story window. Gary takes note and assumes it's the bedroom of the leader. He looks at the surrounding homes as he brainstorms a scheme. The sound of a house door slamming shut can be heard as a neighbor walks outside. Gary snaps out of his scheming trance and starts walking back to the van. The neighbor passes by in their red sports car. Once the car is out of sight, Gary turns back around and steals the mail from the big white house with the punk kids inside. It wasn't his plan but it was something. He stuffs it down his shirt, returns to his van, and drives home excited to have thought of a plan.

On his back patio at his property, Gary lounges in his low to the ground folding chair. He tosses a stack of stolen mail on the lawn chair next to him. He cracks open the tall beer and takes the first refreshing bubbly sip to begin his lunch. The cold beer feels good in his hand as the sun beats down high over his head. There were a few tall trees in the uncut backyard with long old drooping branches that provided cover for a shed tucked away near the tree line. The shed is a rust red color, the paint peeling off and the boards holding it together seemed to twist in opposition to each other. It needs a new roof badly. It is starting to be taken over by ivy. In the middle of the yard is a blue above ground pool with a little white ladder hanging from the side. There's no water in the pool and it looks like it has been that way for a long time as bugs and dirt spots cover the floor of it.

He starts devouring the foul hotdog while he picks up the stack of mail off the adjacent chair, spilling some toppings from his meal onto his shirt, but he doesn't care. One by one he looks at each stolen envelope, deciding if it's worth opening. Most are bills and ads and end up being tossed on the round black charcoal grill Gary has in the middle of his square concrete patio. There is a women's beauty magazine addressed to Mrs. Jackson. He assumes that's the mother of the stupid faced bully. Gary sets it aside on the patio next to his beer. Taking his last bite of hotdog, he twists around in his chair to grab a container of lighter fluid tucked away in a cinder block next to the house. He begins pouring lighter fluid all over the stolen mail he put on the grill, soaking it till the ink bleeds. He feels around in his shirt pocket sifting through the lollipops and he pulls out his lighter. The lighter flicks on with the snap of his thumb, he pauses, mildly amused that this isn't the first thing today he has covered in a flammable liquid and set on fire. Carefully he brings the lighter close to a corner of an envelope and in an instant a wave of flames engulfs the paper as it folds and twists in the heat catching the rest of the mail ablaze.

He stands up to adjust his chair, sliding it back a few inches from the heat. In doing so the chair bumps the magazine and it pushes the beer can over and spills beer all over the patio. Without thinking Gary picks up the wet magazine and throws it while muttering profanities at it. It hits the side of the grill and then falls to the concrete. Gary stands up, picks up the magazine and starts beating it against the flames on the grill over and over as if he is punishing it. Lost in his unwarranted rage, flames and ash disperse and land on the uncut lawn. He hovers over the grill, breathing heavy, closing his eyes to regain composure. He lifts his head, takes a deep breath, and reaches for a lollipop. Once unwrapped he starts enjoying his red cherry sucker and sits back down to check if any beer is left in his can. There is some left, but not a lot. Gary takes a swig of the last drops of his tall boy. As the can descends from its tilted position, he sees a fire burning in the grass over the horizon of his beer. His eyes get big and in a panic he rushes to his backyard hose only a few feet away. He twists the spigot on. The fire did not get too big so he had no trouble putting it out. Frustrated and annoyed he goes back inside while leaving his beer can, hot dog container, magazine, and burnt mail remains outside.

In his bedroom he strips down to his briefs and socks and lets gravity drop him on his bed for an afternoon nap. The face down picture frame on the dresser is the focus of Gary's attention as he lays there thinking. Before his mind wanders too far off he forces his eyes shut and rolls over on his side away from the dresser. The sunshine from outside pierces through his thin curtains, providing a warm and cozy nap environment. With anticipation of acting out his plan this evening, he falls asleep hoping to speed up the day and usher in the evening.

Chapter 4

He stretches his arms and legs as he forces open his tired eyes. Groggy and dazed he shifts his legs over the side of the bed and pushes himself up. He rubs his eyes and looks at the clock on his dresser. Wishing more time had passed, he got up to prepare for the night. He slides the closet door open revealing some shirts and coats, most of them looking faded and worn with tattered collars and fraying seams. He scratches his eyebrow with a curled hand as he looks for the perfect shirt for this evening's attire. He grabs a hanger with a navy blue polo and pulls it out to hold it up. He hums a sound of approval and tosses the shirt onto his bed and then digs through his dresser drawer. He searches for a black pair of shorts but can't find any. He does however find a black pair of folded slacks. They look brand new and have only been worn a handful of times on special occasions. He holds them up against his waist and draws an invisible line across the pants with the side of his hand, right above the knee. He throws the pants onto the bed next to the blue shirt and scans the ground looking for his big knife. He kicks at his clothes pile he made from before his nap and finds the knife and holster.

Gary takes his black pants and clips them onto a hanger. He places the hook of the hanger on the headboard of his bed allowing him to pull the slacks taut. With the knife in hand, he begins cutting the slacks right above the knees. The knife is pretty sharp so the task is almost effortless. He slices and saws the pant legs off leaving frayed dangling threads. Once completed he throws the extra material in the corner of his room and unclips the pants from the hanger. He holds the pants once again up to his waist and looks down to examine his work. "Shhhhhoot." he says slowly, realizing he may have cut a little too much off, turning his slacks into very short shorts. He sighs, and tries on his new pair of shorts. He walks into the bathroom and sees that his shorts are very high on his thighs, showing off a lot more of his pasty legs than he would like. Unamused he returns to his bedroom and finishes getting dressed, making sure to put some lollipops in his shirt pocket. Once his shirt, belt, and boots are on he gets on his knees and reaches under the bed. He grabs a worn black empty backpack and tosses his firearm and knife in the bottom of the bag, since his tucked in polo and shorts would not allow for him to properly conceal his weapons.

In the kitchen Gary places his mostly empty and deflated backpack on the table and glances at the clock. With plenty of time to eat dinner before he ventures out, he opens the fridge and grabs another slab of meat identical to what he ate for breakfast. The small mangled cut of meat sizzles and pops as it collides with the filthy cast iron pan. His dead eyes stare at the meat as it cooks and the scent of his meal infiltrates his senses. A few minutes go by and he plates his meal and sits down at his kitchen table. A spacey look comes across his face as he stares down at his plate. With one hand he grabs the steak and squeezes it till his hand tremors. His hair vibrates as he furiously grips the meat, shaking, just as the rage reaches its peak he bites into the cut with his molars and with the force of his whole neck and head rips the meat apart and starts chewing violently. The anger once again flees when the plate is empty. He stacks the plate on the rest of the grimy dishes in the sink, grabs his backpack and makes his way to the backyard.

With the backpack hanging off of one shoulder, Gary starts fumbling with the combination lock on the door to the red shed. As he rotates the dial each way he mumbles the numbers to himself. "Thirty nine, twenty one, thirteen." For a brief moment he is saddened as he clicks the last number on the lock. He pauses and holds the lock in his hand and lets out a deep exhale, then pulls the lock open and opens the creaky door. Gary goes inside the shed only for a few minutes, then returns back outside struggling to zip up his now extremely plump backpack. He locks the shed back up and heads around the side of his yard and hops in his truck laying the backpack on the seat next to him. As he turns the key and waits for the engine to start to life, he glares at the backpack with malice. Once the van is warmed up and ready he makes his way over to Stupid Face Jackson's house.

Dusk arrives as Gary parks his van at the end of the cul-de-sac, keeping a distance but still able to look down the street at his target house. Unwrapping another lollipop Gary rests his head against the headrest and stares out his window toward the house, watching, waiting. As time goes by he watches as car after car fills the dead end road and small groups of teenagers hop out of the cars and enter into the big house. After he has polished off the first lollipop he goes for another, and another, and another. By this time the moon is big and bright against the black sky and Gary sits patiently, waiting for an opportunity.

Finally, the opportunity he was banking on arrives. A dirty red two door truck from the eighties with a bright sign on the top illuminating a popular deep dish pizza franchise *Bottom Feeders* catches Gary's eye as it turns the corner down the cul-de-sac. Without wasting any time, Gary looks in his rear view mirror and runs his hands through his greasy hair a couple times, adjusts the collar of his blue shirt, then grabs his backpack and exits his eye sore of a van. Walking briskly, nearing jogging, Gary makes his way down the sidewalk toward the house keeping an eye on the red truck. The truck seems to slow down as if searching for the correct house numbers for his delivery. The truck loops around the dead end road and makes its way back passing Gary and parks a few houses up from the party. For a moment Gary thought maybe this pizza wasn't going to the house party, but then realized there was no parking for the pizza guy. He continued walking towards the house hoping the pizza was to be delivered to Jake's house. Gary strolls up the driveway and leans his back on the garage waiting to see if the pizza guy will be walking over. The loud music from inside vibrates the garage door as he lurks. In the distance Gary sees the *Bottom Feeders* delivery driver emerge from the glow of a street light. Like an overweight angel descending from the night sky, his blonde hair shimmers in the moonlight underneath his hat to deliver fresh hot pies for drunk teenagers.

Gary waves at the chubby pizza guy until he gets his attention. The man holding the pizza tries to wave back while clamping the boxes of pizza with his chin, but as he waves his foot catches the head of a lawn sprinkler and his body weight lunges him forward. There are a few seconds of him attempting to re-center himself under the pizza but he has no luck. Momentum has taken its course and his whole body collapses onto the front yard. His belly fans out as it crushes the boxes of pizza, his blue shirt ripples and bobs to a halt as he lays there face first in the grass. He slowly stands up, his blue polo wrinkled and out of sorts, and his black shorts now dirty.

"Im...im so sorry." The young man says, horrified and embarrassed. "We are really busy right now but I will get you new pizzas right away. I am so sorry." He says kneeling back down to pick up the flattened boxes.

Gary puts his boot on the box and presses down, crunching more cardboard and preventing the young man from picking up the boxes. He unwraps another lollipop. "How about I just take these...no charge." He says now sucking on the lollipop, looking down on him. The delivery driver looks up, and then down thinking about if he is even allowed to give away this much pizza. Gary notices his hesitation and kneels down to his level with his foot still on the box. "No charge." He says menacingly, glaring daggers through thin strands of black hair. The driver takes a big nervous gulp and nods in agreement. Like a switch Gary's face instantly turns pleasant and he smiles, picking up the flattened and misshaped pizza boxes. "And the hat."

"Why, why do you want my...my hat?" The driver stuttered nervously, confused and ready to get out of there. Looking Gary up and down he noticed they were dressed the same.

Gary just stares blankly and unamused at the man refusing to answer, waiting for him to comply. A few seconds go by and he takes off his blue and black colored hat with the embroidered company logo *Bottom Feeders* on it and hands it to Gary. Gary puts on the hat and brings the bill down, attempting to cover his eyes and keep a low profile. The delivery driver stands back up and briskly walks back to his car, looking over his shoulder several times at the intimidating man who took his hat. Gary scoops up the many boxes of pizza in both arms and rings the front door with his elbow. The music is blasting in the house. Frustrated, he rings the bell repeatedly with his elbow but no one seems to hear the doorbell.

While balancing the pizzas, he reaches down for the doorknob. He struggles to give it a twist with all the boxes he is carrying, but after a couple tries he manages to crack the door open. All at once a plume of scented smoke accompanied by the blasting bass of the music assaults Gary's senses. He winces and scrunches his face. Irritated and annoyed, he enters the party shutting the door behind him with the heel of his boot. He looks around the room in disgust, as every teenager here seems to be already drunk, and there are so many of them. In front of him is a wide set of stairs leading to the second story. On the steps are three highschoolers laughing and being obnoxious as they sip on their red plastic cups. To the left is an open area with some couches and chairs. The area is filled with intoxicated partiers and a ping pong table in the center with red cups at each end. Two ladies are drunkenly throwing ping pong balls overhanded with all their might at the other players' red cups, laughing hysterically as they try to knock over the cups. To the right of the stairs is another open area with a large dining room table positioned under an exquisite chandelier lighting the room. Every chair at the table is filled with a body and a red cup, kids bouncing quarters into a bowl of candy for some sort of drinking game. When the quarter successfully landed in the bowl everyone just yelled and took a drink. None of these games seemed to make sense.

After a few moments of taking in his surroundings, Gary faintly hears someone yell over the music, "Pizza! Woohoo!" Gary looks past the giant dining room table and into the kitchen to see the kid from the convenience store stumble his way over to him carrying a wad of cash in his hand, balancing his body on the backs of chairs as he walks. Gary glares at him, hating everything about him from his buzz cut to his highschool jacket. He doesn't take issue with those things at all, but something about this kid, how he acts, and his stupid face, just makes Gary hate everything about him.

"Hey pizza buddy! I have all your cash right here. I hope it's enough." The drunk teenager says as he holds up a wad of hundred dollar bills and starts stuffing it into Gary's shirt pocket.

Gary looks down at his pocket and back at the kid, "You're a little short."

"Hol..hold on pizza buddy, I.. I know where my parents ka-keep some cash on hand." He replied, stuttering and tripping over his words.

He turns around and makes his way up the stairs, leaning heavily on the rail for balance.

Gary stands at the foot of the stairs awkwardly holding the pizzas observing the madness that is his surroundings. After a minute or two the kid returns holding a handful of more hundred dollar bills and he stuffs it into Gary's shirt pocket, which is now bulging and overflowing with money. Gary looks down again at his pocket, then back at the kid, and then holds the tattered boxes out towards him.

"Bro, are these boxes supposed to look like this?" He asks as he grabs the boxes.

"They're recycled boxes or something, it's fine." Gary assured him. "Hey, may I use your restroom?" He asks the kid who sways and tries to balance the stack of uneven boxes.

"Oh yea, anything for my fly guy bringing the hot pies." He said as he brushes past Gary heading for the dining room table.

"Where is it?" Gary yells back, but he is given no response as the music is blaring and he didn't hear him. He rolls his eyes, looks around and as he is about to make his way up the stairs, out of the corner of his eye he notices the kid swaying and leaning more as he walks. Gary watches the kid fall over onto the pizza boxes, smashing them before he is able to put them on the table. The room roars with laughter as the drunks howl and point at the kid. Gary raises his eyebrows in disbelief that in one night he watched two different people fall on the same boxes of pizza. He adjusts his hat and keeps his head down as he makes his way upstairs, weaving through the laughing kids hanging out in his way.

At the top of the stairs he pauses, looking left, then right trying to figure out which way his room is located. With his previous knowledge of where he saw the kid from outside through the window, he turns to the right and makes his way around to a hallway. He walks down the hallway with his backpack on and stops at the first door he encounters.

Slowly he grabs and turns the doorknob and cracks the door open and peeks inside. A quick look into the room reveals three young ladies drunkenly gossiping in the back corner while passing a bottle of liquor. They don't seem to notice Gary as he quickly glances around the study, looking at the big polished wooden desk and the big leather chair. He sees book shelves on the left hand wall filled with various books on Law. Seeing that this is not the room he is looking for he quietly closes the door and moves on down the hall.

He sees pictures of the Jackson family hanging up as he walks to the next room. Every picture looks professionally taken, the family all dressed up for each photo. Gary approaches the next door to his left and puts his hand on the door knob and brings his ear in close to see if he can hear anything over the loud music. A faint sound can be heard on the other side. It almost sounds like yelling. With curiosity and caution, he cracks open the door and pokes his head in to find a jock in a letterman jacket kneeling over the toilet vomiting. Gary's face curls in disgust and he slams the door shut. He keeps walking to the last door on the right.

Again he opens the door and peeks through the sliver of a gap to find a bedroom with the light left on. Once he notices that it is empty ,he slithers between the tight door gap and shuts the door promptly behind him. He scans the room which is surprisingly neat and tidy for a highschool boy, but his parents probably run a tight ship he thought to himself, based on what he has seen of this family so far. There are posters of football players on the wall, a desk with some notebooks on it, a small entertainment center with a TV and the latest video game console hooked up to it, a big closet with sliding brown wooden doors, and on the dresser next to his bed is a signed football in a glass case. His interest peaked, Gary walks and examines what he can only imagine is a prized possession. The signature reads, *To Jake*, then underneath is an illegible scribble he is unable to make out who signed it.

While standing next to Jake's bed, Gary swings his backpack off his shoulder and sets it on the bed. He unzips the front pocket and rummages through it and pulls out a yellow stud finder, a flat rectangular woodworking pencil, a hammer, and finally a clear plastic case filled with large nails. The nails and hammer he leaves on top of the backpack and he takes the stud finder and pencil to the wall behind him with the window facing the street. He closes the blinds and holds the stud finder up to the wall and presses down the button, no light or noise omits from the device. With a couple of smacks to the side of the yellow plastic tool and a few more intense pushes of the button the stud finder remains quiet. His breathing intensifies as he flips over the stud finder and opens the back, revealing there are no batteries in it. Pinching the bridge of his nose and closing his eyes he takes a deep breath to calm his emotions. Once composed he starts looking around the room for any solutions. He walks over to the entertainment center and starts examining its contents. He finds a video game controller and retrieves the batteries from it and puts them into his stud finder.

He returns to the wall and presses the stud finder against it and taps on the button. A red light glows as he drags the device sideways against the textured wall. As he drags it the light turns green over one of his sports posters, Gary takes the pencil from his shirt pocket and makes a straight vertical line. He repeats this process to find the other side of the stud inside the wall and makes another mark on the poster. He finds another stud on this wall before moving to the wall behind Jake's bed. His foot sinks into the mattress as he props himself up onto this bed, standing on top with his dirty boots The stud finder light glows green as it finds another stud right above the bed. He hops off the bed and repeats this process on every wall of the room, finding every stud he can. Once finished locating the hidden beams in the large bedroom, he pulls out another lollipop to savor.

He returns to the side of the bed, slides the case of nails and hammer off his backpack and onto the bed and slowly unzips the main pocket on the backpack. As he does, a horrendous thick rotting stench permeates the air. However, Gary is unphased by such unpleasantness. In fact, he barely even notices it. He reaches his hand into the bag and his fingers grip a moist, scraggly, dirty tuft of hair, and he pulls out a dead possum. He brings the carcass up to eye level holding the dead animal by the back of the neck. Dried patches of hardened blood coat the fur of this creature. As Gary stares into its dead eyes his lips tighten, his grip follows suit as fury finds its way back to Gary. He takes the hammer and nails in one hand and shuffles over to the first stud markings he made on the wall next to the window and forcefully slams the dead possum right between the pencil marks on the poster. With a dexterous hand he flips open the case while still holding the hammer and manages to slide a nail over the edge of the container and takes it out of the case with his teeth. He closes the case and puts it in his front pant pocket, then lines the nail up to the throat of the critter. In sync with the music he hammers away at the nail. The strikes of the hammer are veiled by the bass drum from the dance music blasting downstairs. The resistance of the nail changes as it makes its way through various dead tissue, then the drywall, then the wood. A dead possum is now fastened to Jake's wall. Stepping back, he takes a moment to admire his work. He moves on to the next stud but not before hatefully spitting on the possum.

"You'll be in good company with this dirt bag Jake, a match made in heaven." He says with a scowl.

Another possum is taken out of the backpack. This one seems to have been dead for much longer. It has black rot bordering missing patches of skin and muscle. His slender fingers grasp another nail and he stands on top of Jake's bed and hammers another possum into the wall to the beat of the music. As he turns around and bends over to grab another possum from his bag, the possum he just hung slides off the nail. The rotten flesh rips out from the nail and the possum bounces off Gary's lower back and onto the pillow. With an angry grunt he picks up the fallen possum and this time drives the large nail through its skull making sure this time it sticks. He hops off the bed and leaves behind a little dirt from his boots to go along with some possum fur and rotting sludge that now resides on Jake's pillow. Gary hangs up a total of six possums around the room, each one dirty with varying degrees of decay with their thin stringy tails dangling still and lifelessly.

He puts the tools back in the bag with one remaining possum he hasn't used yet. His hand digs down to the bottom of the backpack underneath the last possum to grab a bundled up pelt-like object. He flattens it out and puts his hand through an opening at the bottom to open it up. He takes his *Bottom Feeders* hat off and puts it in the backpack. Holding his black greasy hair back he tilts his head down, spits out his lollipop stick, and puts on his homemade fuzzy mask. It's composed of several old tattered possum pelts of various shades of grays and browns sewn together with thick black thread. The mask surrounds Gary's entire head and face. Two crudely cut eye holes are the only windows of the pelt mask that he can see through. Seven dangling gray possum tails are stitched around the horrifying mask on the upper sides, encircling his head like a crown. He turns the light off and hides in Jake's closet.

He peers through the tiny wooden slats from inside the closet, looking into the dark empty room. His eyes adjust to the low light as he waits. Several hours go by and Gary is still waiting patiently in the closet, the music downstairs is still going, however it's volume has been reduced significantly from what it was earlier. His foot shakes as he tries to hold it. He didn't expect to have to wait this long. As he taps his foot, he contemplates what he should do. Relieve himself in the closet or risk being seen going to the bathroom. After a few minutes of wiggling uncomfortably Gary slowly slides open the closet door and walks through the bedroom to the door. Putting his ear to the door he checks if the coast is clear. He doesn't hear anybody so he gently pushes the door open. The light from the hallway reveals the ugliness of his possum tailed mask as he looks both ways down the hallway, the tails swinging side to side as he does.

He enters the bathroom and closes the door behind him, the jock now passed out slouched over the toilet seat. Now wiggling violently Gary walks over to the jock and tries to assess if he can aim the stream around his head. It would be close. He decides to find another option. The sink looks promising but it's fairly shallow, too much splash risk he thought to himself. Instead he steps over the passed out kid and disappears behind the shower curtain into the tub. Quickly he unzips and relieves himself right into the drain of the shower. He lets out a sigh of relief as he rests his head on the back of his neck. The urine starts coming back out of the clogged drain. Just as he is finishing up the door swings open and makes a loud slamming noise as it hits the wall.

Two young ladies stumble into the bathroom. "You're almost there Wilma, you can…." One of the ladies said as she carried her friend on her shoulder. Her sentence was interrupted by an obnoxious belch. "…do it." She said, slurring her words to her friend as she helped her get into the bathroom.

"Rob, you silly, that…is…not a bed, we need to use that." She said to the passed out jock as the two swayed back and forth.

As this is happening Gary instantly recoils into the corner of the shower with his back to the wall, trying not to stand where he just peed.

"Here, just go there." As she says this a head peers through the shower curtain, her long brown hair covering her face. Gary is remarkably still, trying not to draw any attention his way. The girl lets out a sickening burp, immediately followed by a strong and explosive stream of flowing vomit, chunks of pepperoni, beer, and stomach acid. She yaks a second time, and a third, and now the vomit is slowly making its way towards Gary's boots. In a panic Gary muenevers himself with one foot on each edge of the tub as the horrible sounds of a sick vomiting teenager continues in front of him with a river of chunky belly juices becoming a class three rapid right beneath him. His hands grip the shower curtain for balance as he watches this scene unfold. Finally all the juices have left her body and all that remains are the disgusting throaty sounds of dry heaving. Just when he thinks she's all done, her friend's head pops through the shower curtain right next to her, her long red curly hair touching the floor of the bathtub as she projectile vomits on the wall and then down into the tub. Now there are two girls and one tub, filled with puke and urine. Gary's stomach turns at the sight, smell, and sound of gagging. Eventually the nightmare ends and the girls stop, their hair holding on to some slimy chunks as their heads disappear to the other side of the shower curtain. He listens as the two stand up and begin to exit the bathroom, but not before they clumsily trip over the passed out jock. One of them slams against the wall as she falls, the other catches herself on the door knob and pulls herself up and out of the bathroom. Gary peeks around the shower curtain and watches the fallen girl on her knees crawl out of the bathroom like a big drunk baby, her eyes barely open and drool forming at the sides of the mouth like a dog. As she crawls, a small vomit trail is being left behind her by her red hair dragging on the floor. Relieved that this episode is all over he grabs the shower curtain with both hands and tries to climb down off the tub's ledge. He puts too much weight on the rod and it snaps off the wall and he falls back against the wall and tumbles and slips into the vomit and urine filled tub. The juices slide into his short shorts and it covers his legs as he flails in disgust.

He hoists himself up on the edge of the tub and rolls out, accidently kicking the jock in the head with his boot as he lands on his back behind him. The kid's head falls in the toilet and there is an audible crack as his chin hits the inside of the porcelain bowl. Gary stands up and puts two hands on the boy's shoulders and pulls him away from the toilet and against the wall. His chin is split and bleeding. Gary takes off his smelly polo with vomit stains and wraps it from the bottom of the kid's chin to the top of his head and ties the makeshift tourniquet off. Now shirtless, with a tattered possum mask and throw up covered short shorts, Gary returns to the closet with an empty bladder and continues to wait.

About an hour goes by when through the slits of the closet paneling, Gary sees the bedroom door fling open, the hallway light illuminating the bedroom. Gary squints as his eyes adjust and he sees Jake Jackson, the stupid faced kid stumbling in through the door way. Jake is holding the hand of a blond girl as she stumbles in behind him. They shut the door and drunkenly make their way to the bed and start making out. An audience of dead possums and Gary watch and listen in the dark. Before things get too uncomfortable for Gary, he reaches for his bag on the ground and pulls out the last possum and his big knife from the bottom of his backpack. With the blade of his knife he sticks it through the space between the door and the frame and slides the closet open slowly and quietly. He steps into the middle of the room, staring at the couple who still hasn't noticed him. An amused smile cracks behind the tattered mask as he positions himself at the edge of the bed. He looms directly over the drunken couple who are still unaware of Gary's presence. He raises the possum carcass with one hand high above the two teens, and with his knife drives it into the upper torso of the dead animal. With one quick downward motion of the knife he rips the animal open. Blood and entrails start sliding out of the possum as Gary shakes the creature up and down trying to dislodge the innards. He waits for them to notice the bloody mess dripping onto them but they keep making out. Shaking the possum even harder now, he starts cutting away at the innards as rotted black slimy organs fall on Jake and his date. The teens still don't notice anything. In a pouting fashion Gary slaps his hands against his sides. The teens are spreading the dark red, half clotted possum blood on each other and they still haven't opened their eyes or seem to have felt any of the organs on them. Aloof to their surroundings, they continue to moan and engage in their adult activity. Frustrated Gary puts the possum and knife on the dresser and grabs the chair at Jake's desk. He carries it back to the side of the bed and takes a seat next to the couple. He grabs the possum he just gutted and slides his hand into it like a puppet. He manipulates it to face him and wiggles it around, quietly grunting he pretends the possum is talking to him. Gary nods and the possum tails on his mask sway in agreement. He continues this deranged puppet show, making the possum's grunting get louder and louder with each interaction but still the couple is oblivious and now their shirts are coming off.

She flings hers off and it lands right on top of Gary's head covering his mask. He pulls it off and throws it across the room. He leans in towards the bed and brings his puppet up to Jake's cheek. Gary begins making kissing noises as he rubs the possums gory head against his face. Finally the moment Gary has been waiting for, a reaction. Jake pushes the girl off of himself and instinctively jerks his head away from the moist rough pelt. His eyes take a minute to focus in the dark as he stares in the direction that he felt the uncomfortable object on his face. Enough moonlight creeps through the blinds on the window to showcase a man in a grotesquely stitched possum mask, with two sharp beady eyes staring at him as he holds a bloody possum puppet.

Jake screams a high pitched scream of pure fright. The girl screams as a reaction to Jake's screaming but then quickly realizes what he is yelling about. She screams again, louder and more shrill than her first cry. In a panic they scurry off the bed falling to the ground. They stand up and try to get to the door but Gary snaps to his feet and rushes to the door. He blocks the door and holds the possum out, now gripping it by the head. The couple screams as Gary tightens his grip on the head of the creature. His entire arm up to his shoulder shakes as he squeezes tightly.   All of a sudden the skull gives way and a horrendous, unforgettable crunching sound omits from his fingers as his fist tightens. The skull is crushed in his grip and some ooze squirts out from between his fingers. Their screams continue and Gary holds his knife up to his mask, resting it on where his lips would be signaling them to quiet down. He takes a step to the side of the door allowing them to get through. Jake and the blonde girl are frozen in fear. Jake tries to say something but can't seem to speak, just some gasps and a few audible yelps come out as he trembles before the masked man. Gary slowly brings the knife down just below shoulder height, holding it out to the side. Disguising his voice to be low and slow, with a monster-like growl he says, "Do you like...what I...have done with the place?" He flicks the lightswitch on with his knife. The bloody possum carcasses hanging on the wall, now seen for the first time by their intended audience. The kids scream when they see all the dead animals, and scream again when they notice each other is covered in smears of thick dark blood. Gary takes another step to the side of the door, with both hands and he points to the door, giving them a subtle bow, giving them the ok to leave. The ghostly pale teens hesitate to move past the ugly masked menace. Gary remains as still as a statue still bowing, waiting for them to pass through. After a few seconds the girl makes a run for it and trembles and shakes as she fumbles with the doorknob and zips past Gary. Seeing her pass safely, Jake gets the courage to for it and makes a run for the door. As Jake passes Gary, Gary quickly holds out the dead possum and starts shoving it in Jake's face. He screams and falls against the door frame and Gary pins him and smothers him with the animal. Jake eventually breaks free from Gary and continues to bolt down the hallway, coughing up hair as he runs. As he turns the corner he begins projectile vomiting off the balcony, grabbing on to the guard rail as he moves down the stairs.

Gary closes the door and walks over to Jake's bed. He pulls back the covers on his bed and places the possum puppet onto the bed. With its head on the pillow he brings the covers back up and tucks the critter in. Beneath his feet is Jake's letterman jacket. He picks it up and puts it on. He then rushes to the closet and grabs his backpack and puts his knife inside. He gets behind the blinds and unlocks and opens the window and the summer air rushes in. In the corner of his eye he sees the football encased in glass sitting on the wooden dresser. He snatches the signed football from the case and throws it out the window. He then twists through the window and grabs on to the window sill with both hands, now dangling from a second story window.

His fingers grip tight as he looks down at some bushes beneath his feet. He takes a deep breath and releases his grip. The bush engulfs him and he rolls out the side into some bark dust. He reaches his hand back into the bush and pulls out the football and holds it close as he makes his way back to his van in the very early hours of the morning, still dark, with his new letterman jacket and football. Screams can still be heard from inside the house.

Chapter 5

His eyelids struggle to crack open as he rolls on his side, trying to get his tired eyes to focus on the blurry numbers on the alarm clock. Well into the afternoon Gary finally forces himself up and dangles his legs over the bed while rubbing his face. Bits of dried blood and hair are stained into the white sheets. A few leaves and twigs from the bush under Jake's window are still stuck on the letterman jacket Gary fell asleep in. He takes off the jacket and throws it on the floor next to the stolen football.

Dirty and sweaty with dried vomit on his shorts, Gary takes a shower and cleans up. Another day means another meal with a small slab of steak from the refrigerator. Exhausted and groggy, his head heavy, Gary snags a six pack of cheap beer and some lollipops and sits out on his creaky front porch in an even more creaky old wooden chair. He breaks off one of the beers from the plastic vine and puts the rest on the small round wooden table next to him. The warm air feels good against his bare arms. He squints as the sun shines down. He pulls the tab, it cracks open and cold foam pours down the can and a few drops of brew dribble onto his white tank top.

The beautiful scenery is not enough for Gary to appreciate it as he gazes out onto the field. Even after the excitement from the previous night, his soul feels dull and numb. Another weekend alone with some beer and no one to share it with. It used to bother him but after many years of the continued solitude, he grew accustomed to the quietness of his life. And then after he became accustomed, he became numb. The day to day chores and the demands of labor to put food on the table for only himself ate away at him, going through the motions just to survive on auto pilot. He wasn't completely gone to himself and void of feeling, he still had anger and he had a cold beer sweating into his hand.

Three beers later, Gary sees in the far distance two bicyclists riding on the main road. He watches them peddle up the slight incline, their bodies pushed forward onto the handlebars as they stand up on their bikes peddling. To Gary's surprise they turn onto his dirt driveway and are making their way towards his house. He takes a sip of his beer and places it on the wooden table. He leans forward and reaches behind his back and pulls out his pistol and sets it on the table as well, just in case. He unwraps a lollipop and holds it behind his teeth, biting on the stem, his eyes following the bikes.

As they ride closer Gary narrows his eyes to focus his vision. He notices that it is two young boys riding on the bikes. Puzzled and trying to figure out who they are and why they are here, he crosses his arms and leans back in his chair, scowling. They peddle past the gopher van and stop a few feet from the porch.

"We brought you money." The younger looking boy says waving a white envelope in front of himself.

"For what." Gary said sharply, his eyes cold, his mouth tightens around the lollipop.

"For killing all the gophers. Our mom had us ride over to give you the rest of the money." The older kid chimed in.

It took him a second but eventually he recognized the kids from a few days ago.

Leaning back in his chair, Gary puts his elbow on the arm rest and slowly rotates his wrist until his palm is facing upward. Kyle climbs off his bike and lets it fall in the dirt and walks up to the porch. Kyle watches Gary as he climbs the steps, each foot creates a dry creaky noise as the steps bow beneath him. At the top of the porch Kyle pauses, he sees the gun and cautiously leans forward keeping his feet planted trying to put the envelope in Gary's hand, not wanting to get closer than he has to. The envelope hovers a few inches in front of Gary's fingers, in reach for him to grab it but he doesn't. His beading eyes just stare down at Kyle as he stretches his arm forward, struggling to get the envelope in his hand. Kyle loses his balance and his arms helicopter around in circles as he tries to center himself. He stumbles a few steps towards Gary and drops the envelope on the porch. He turns around in a mild panic and jumps off the porch, leaping over the steps.

Gary leans down and scoops up the envelope. His slender fingers open the flap and he flips through the bills with his thumb. He slips the envelope under the gun and grabs his beer. The chair creaks as he leans back and takes another refreshing sip. Cody, still standing over his bike, begins to turn it around to head back down the driveway. Kyle hears Cody handling his bike and turns around. Cody looks back and motions for his little brother to come on. Kyle turns back around towards Gary.

"Do you need any help trapping gophers today?" Kyle asks.

Gary, sensing the hope in his voice, gulps down the rest of the beer and places the empty can next to the other ones and snaps off another beer from the plastic. "No".

Kyle's shoulders and back dip in disappointment. His eagerness was replaced by defeat and Gary noticed immediately.

"I need help checking the traps." He said hoping to lift the kids spirits back up.

A rush of energy enters back into Kyle. He perks up and his eyes grow as wide as his smile. Cody however, does not share his brother's excitement. But it was summer and they had nothing else really to do so he went along with it to make his brother happy.

He chugs the rest of his mostly full can of beer and lets out a large muffled belch, trying to mute it the best he can with a closed mouth. "Meet me around back."

With a burst of energy, Kyle runs around the side of the house as Cody reluctantly drops his bike to the ground and follows behind. Gary goes to his van and grabs his shotgun and an open box of shells and heads to the backyard. They boys sit on some chairs and wait for Gary on the back patio. Gary rounds the corner and without saying anything walks past the brothers towards the tree line assuming that they would follow. Turning around he sees the brothers staring at him, waiting for their next command. Gary rolls his eyes and shouts for them to come on. They scurry up to Gary who then gives Kyle the box of shotgun shells to hold and the three of them head into the trees.

It was a quiet walk, only the sounds of the birds chirping and the leaves dancing in the wind could be heard. But after a few minutes of walking, Kyle broke the silence, "Do you live out here alone?"

Gary looked at Kyle, surprised by such a personal question, then looked back ahead. "Yes", he answered.

"Have you always been alone?" He asked, Cody giving him a good punch on the shoulder.

"Kyle!" Cody whispers in a loud rebuke.

Gary remains quiet for a few moments, processing all the emotions rising to the surface. His face shifts and he winces as he struggles to decide if he wants to answer the question. He isn't used to such questions, no one asks because no one cares. Now there is a kid who for the second time, is stirring up all sorts of emotions.

"We bought this property right after we got married many years ago. She worked from home as a writer, and in her free time loved to garden. She used to live in an apartment and never got to have a garden of her own till we got here. But she always loved the idea that she could nurture something as small as a seed and help it grow into a large tomato vine or a giant zucchini. She was one with nature you could say. Anyways, she worked hard on the garden, poured everything into it. Onions, zucchini, potatoes, carrots, tomatoes, she planted everything she could. But before any of the food was ready to be picked, it would be taken. Tomatoes would be green then gone, the zucchini was destroyed before it was big enough to pick, even the root vegetables were dug up by something. It made her so mad she told me I needed to do something about it. I said sure honey I'll put out some traps and see if we catch anything. So I did just that. I put out a couple of metal cages, one way in no way out sort of a deal, and put some vegetables in there. When we checked the traps the next day, each trap had a possum in it. We were excited to hopefully have found the culprits and I drove the two possums far from our property and let them loose. We set the traps again that same day just to see if there were any more out there. Sure enough the next day two more possums were stuck in the traps, and again we drove them far away. This went on for about a week before I decided to set more traps. I couldn't believe how many possums we had caught in a week. I set out five additional traps, and sure enough every single one was full the next day. This was driving her insane, they just kept coming. She decided the traps weren't enough and maybe that the possums we let go were finding their way back here. I told her that's impossible. She started to go out at night after dinner once the sun set and hunt for them with this very shotgun. I never went with her, the traps seemed to be doing their job. Most nights her endeavors were fruitless, but on a rare occasion I could hear a blast in the distance, and sometimes she would come back home with one of them suckers. She started staying out later, and later, and later, obsessed with finding them all. One night she didn't come home till the morning. I was brewing some coffee when she walked in the back door. She said she thinks she knows what to do now and went to bed. I went to work like I normally do. But when I came home I found her in the bottom of the swimming pool with the possums we caught the night before. She had apparently emptied out all the water from our pool and was now sitting in it with a bunch of disease carrying rodents. I asked her if she had lost her mind. She just said I wouldn't understand. That evening during dinner, I noticed some bite marks on her arm. I confronted her on them and she passed it off as nothing. Every day I would come home from work and she would be in the pool with the possums. Every day a few more would be in there. I think she just went crazy. The last night I saw her I was drinking a beer and watching some TV and she came into the living room with a box filled with old junk, plates, cups, silverware, some rope, tools and all sorts of crap from the garage. She said she needs to help them. I looked at her like she was crazy and asked what are you talking about. I told her she needs to see a doctor and we are making an appointment tomorrow. She just walked out the back door towards the trees and I never saw her again."

Both Kyle and Cody had their heads down as they listened intently. Kyle looked up. "What happened to all the possums in the pool?"

Gary raised the shotgun, "I shot every single one of them and left their bodies to rot in that pool."

Kyle could see the water collecting at the corners of Gary's eyes. Gary was doing everything in his power to hold back the tears.

"What was her name?" Kyle asked.

"Charlotte," Gary paused after saying the name, realizing he hadn't said it out loud in years ever since her disappearance. "The only thing she left me was a note on the fridge. It had coordinates on it."

"Coordinates?" Kyle asked.

"Yeah, like numbers on a map, a location." Gary replied softly, trying not to choke on his words.

"Where is the location?" Kyle asked.

Gary stopped in his tracks. In front of them was a slight hill with thick brush spanning wide and tall, much taller than any of them. Thorns and barbs and tangled branches densely covered the hillside.

"Right here. When I came looking for her she moved most of the traps to this area. I think she thought that's where they were coming from."

He continued walking along the brushy hillside and pointed out one of the traps at the base of the hill. Inside was a sniveling little possum with its beady eyes looking up at the three of them. They approached the cage, looming over it, Kyle started to get nervous but excited, ready to prove himself. Cody was uncomfortable, and Gary was disgusted with the sight before him. Gary looks at the boys and taps on his ear then points to the box of shotgun shells. Kyle looks in the box and finds a handful of loose ear plugs and passes them out. Gary stretches his hand out, signaling for Kyle to hand him the box. As Kyle places the box in Gary's hand, Gary passes the shotgun to Kyle. A big smile stretches across his face as he takes a few steps back from the cage and brings the firearm to his shoulder. His stance is unstable and the gun wobbles as he tries to control it. His cheek presses against the stock and his teeth clench, his determination beams from his eyes. He takes a deep breath and pulls the trigger. *Click.* He flinches but nothing happens. He turns to Gary to find him standing with his arms crossed, holding up a shell between his fingers shaking it back and forth. He tosses the shell to Kyle and points to the gun where to put it. He inserts the shell and returns the firearm to his shoulder. The possum looks right up the barrel at Kyle. He freezes and clears his throat. He doesn't know if he can do it with the creature looking back at him. Gary walks next to Kyle and kneels down. "These things ruined my life. Don't feel anything for them. They are cancer, they are diseases, they are demons, they are possums."

In an instant Kyle's whole body tenses up, and he pulls the trigger. The blast rips pellets through the possum's face tearing away at its skull and fur. Blood splashes back in a flash coating the ground around and in the cage. It drops dead instantly. He feels relieved that the anticipation is over and that he actually did it. Gary stands back up and puts his hand on the boy's shoulder. "Next time, don't think about it, just shoot it."

The brothers walk closer to the cage and look at what is left of the body.

"Now what?" Cody asks, unknowingly holding his turning stomach.

"Grab it outta there and let's head to the next one." Gary said, a hint of delight in his voice. Delighted in knowing Cody would hate carrying it, and delighted in Kyle and his determination.

"I'm not touching that thing!" Cody shouted back.

Gary walked up to the cage pushing Kyle to the side. He knelt down to Cody's level. Looking into Gary's eyes was like looking at an oncoming storm. There was a wildness and rage beneath his piercing pupils.

"Let me tell you something boy." He said as a heavy breath exhales through his nostrils.

"In these woods, you…" A bony pencil-like finger shoves into the boy's chest. "…are a harvester of evil." He looks into the cage and opens it up, pulling the dead bloody possum out and holding it up by its tail. "And the crop is ready." Paraylzed by fear, Cody stands there dumbfounded. He tries to speak but only a squeak comes out. He brings the possum close to his face. "Now take it." Cody quickly grabs the tail and as he does his face curls in disgust. A smile sweeps across Gary's face, "See, that wasn't so hard." He stands up and starts walking, following the brush line at the base of the hill towards the next trap.

The events at the other traps were similar to the first. Gary would point out the trap location, Kyle would load in a shell and blast the possum to smithereens, and Cody would reluctantly grab the possums out of the trap. By the end, Cody was carrying seven dead possums like firewood, his arms out with his palms up, and carcasses stacked on top of each other.

After the last kill they all head back to the house. Cody drops the stack of possums on the back patio with a sigh of relief. He looks down at his shirt and it's spotted with dirt and blood. Kyle hands the shotgun back to Gary. Gary nods and a smile sneaks past his resting grim face, quietly proud of him. Before putting the shotgun away he bends down and pulls out his knife from his ankle holster and hands it to Kyle handle first. His little hands grip the knife handle. Curious, he asks, "What's this for?"

"Take their skin off." He told him nonchalantly, as normal a tone as saying good morning to someone. Without any further instruction he walked inside with the gun and box of shells. A few moments later he returned outside to the brothers. He brought out Jake's signed football and his letterman jacket. Kyle was on his knees, bent over a possum, digging and twisting the knife into the possum skin, trying to pry it off like a crowbar. Amused at this sight Gary watched Kyle struggle for a few moments before stepping in to help. He kneels down next to Kyle, sets the football and jacket down, and takes the knife from him. "Like this." A few skillful cuts later and he was peeling off the skin. He looks at Cody and smiles. "You wanna try?" Cody shook his head no, closing one eye trying not to look. Gary gives the knife back to Kyle, "You do the rest." Kyle nodded. He had never had this kind of responsibility before. Carrying and shooting guns, now skinning his game, he felt accomplished.

"Why don't you start stacking some coals up on the grill." He says to Cody, pointing at a half full bag of charcoal by the back door. Cody listens and grabs the bag and starts stacking the charcoal on the grill. Gary continus to coach Kyle in skinning the possums on the patio. Once all the skin was removed, he then instructed him on how to cut the meat off.   Gary took some slices off of one and had Kyle watch. He made it seem effortless. His cuts perfect, his technique flawless, he made it seem like an artform. With the knife now in Kyle's hand, his attempts were less precise. His cuts looked rough and jagged and he struggled a bit to get as much meat off the creature than Gary. Gary coached him through cutting up the rest of the possums, the skins stacked in one pile on the patio, the meat in another.

Gary stands back to his feet and sees the pile of coals Cody made. He used the whole half of the bag which was way too many. Feeling a rare stroke of compassion for another's mistake, he didn't confront Cody. Instead he laid the letterman jacket on the coals with the football on top. "Lighter fluid." He said to Cody, pointing to a cinder block with a container of lighter fluid tucked away inside. Cody grabs it and goes to give it to Gary. Gary refuses to take it and signals Cody to do it. Finally something Cody would enjoy on this day. He smiled and started dousing the coals in fluid. As the lighter fluid kept pouring, Gary would look at him, then back at the coals, wondering how much he was going to use. The jacket and the football were completely soaked, every coal glistened. There was more than plenty of fluid but now Gary was just curious on how much he was going to use. The entire container of lighter fluid was now empty. A couple of more shakes just to make sure every drop was out, then Cody gives a thumbs up to Gary. Gary just rolls his eyes and pulls out some matches from his pocket. Leaning back and turning his head away from the grill he strikes the match. The brothers notice Gary's caution and they each take a big step back. With a flick of the wrist the match flies into the coals and with a roar a wall of flames stretches high into the air.

Gary went back inside and brought out an extra wooden chair from the front porch, a six pack of beer and a two liter bottle of off brand soda. The three of them sit around the inferno and Gary passes Kyle the bottle of soda and hands out some lollipops from his front pocket. Kyle and Cody look uncomfortably at the soda and lollipops, as if a moral quandary was before them.

"That's a soda, and that's a lollipop, you drink that…" Gary said facetiously, pointing at the soda. "…and you eat that." He said pointing to the lollipop. Gary is dumbfounded that a couple of kids get their hands on a bountiful amount of tooth rotting sugar and they sit there as if they were handed a bag of vegetables.

"Mom doesn't let us drink soda or eat candy. She says sugar is bad." Cody informed Gary, holding his lollipop with a disappointed expression on his face.

"What does your mom think about you riding your bikes to a stranger's house, who then lets you use his gun to kill wild animals and then skin em on his back porch to eat them?" He leans back and crosses his arms. "I could kill you faster than sugar." The boys ponder this and look at each other. In a simultaneous agreement, they each unwrap their lollipops and enjoy the sweet juicy fruity flavor. Kyle then proceeds to twist open the big bottle.

"Do you have a cup?" He asks, trying to balance the heavy bottle on his knee.

Gary tears a beer from the plastic and cracks it open. "I ain't using a cup, why should you?"

Kyle pauses, attempting to read Gary whether he is kidding or not. He then lifts the bottle to his lips and starts chugging the soda. The weight is too much for Kyle and the bottle slips and soda floods his nose and pours all over his shirt. Amused, Gary sips on his beer. Cody snatches the bottle out from Kyle's hand and starts drinking.

The flames from the grill subside and the smoke from the coals take its place. A few minutes of silence pass as they sit waiting for the coals to be ashy. It was against Gary's nature to inquire about personal issues but he felt compelled to return the kindness Kyle showed him through his interest in his life earlier in the woods. He clears his throat with a few grunts and washes down the uneasiness with a swig of beer.

"So...eh...what do kids do for fun these days?" He said, focusing on his beer can.

With great enthusiasm Kyle piped up, "video games!" Cody smiled and nodded in agreement.

Gary scoffed. "Your mom will let you play video games but she won't let you have candy? Sure, let's save the precious teeth but let the brain rot away."

The brothers just shrugged their shoulders not really sure what to do or say.

Gary continued. "Let me ask you something." He leaned forward holding his beer in both hands, his black hair draping down over his eye. "Is your mom fat?"

The brothers looked wildly confused at the question. They glanced at each other, not sure how to respond. Kyle, trying to be careful with his words, says in a sheepish manner, "I guess, maybe a little, I don't know." He wishes to respect his mother but remain truthful. Cody again shrugged his shoulders not wishing to partake.

"Well that solves that mystery. You see, your mom doesn't want you to end up like her, so she tells you you're not allowed to have sugar. But I'm willing to bet money that if you snoop around her room, look in her dresser or closet, you're gonna find boxes of cookies and candy." He leans back again and takes another sip and wipes his mouth with the back of his hand. "Is your gym teacher fat?" He asks the brothers. Both brothers smile and laugh nodding their heads up and down. "Same thing." He continues. "They don't wanna put in the work to be healthy themselves, so they use their body as a teaching tool. *Do your pushups or you'll end up like me."*

The kids laughed, which in turn made Gary laugh. Something he hasn't done in a long time.

"How do the coals look, Cody?

"I don't know."

Gary rubs his eyebrows in annoyance. "How about you stand up and look?"

He climbs out of his chair and looks at the coals. "They are turning white."

"Why don't you throw some of that meat on there." He said pointing to the pile on the ground.

Cody scrunches his nose and shakes his head no. Kyle excitedly jumps out of his chair and darts over to the pile of meat and picks up a slab.

"There's dirt on it." He said holding the possum meat up with two fingers.

Gary tears away another beer from the plastic and underhand tosses it to Kyle. He drops the meat and catches the beer. "Clean off the meat, just rinse 'em off."

One by one Kyle rinses off the possum meat with beer and throws them on the grill. Each one sizzles and pops as it hits the hot surface. Kyle sits back down with a big smile on his face, excited to eat the creatures they caught.

"So um...what does your dad do?" He asks uncomfortably, returning to his blank gaze towards his beer can.

The two brothers' faces deflated. They didn't need to say anything. Gary could tell something happened and he was no longer around. He felt bad for them, and then angry for them. His beer began to wrinkle and pop as his grip tightened around it.

"Where is he?" His tone now lowered, trying to hide the anger that so quickly took over.

"One day he just never came home from work. It happened a long time ago. We never met him, just seen pictures." Cody said, reaching for the bottle of soda.

"Well I guess technically I met him, but I was too little to remember."

"What line of work was he in?" Gary asked.

Cody in the middle of a big swig from the bottle starts coughing and spitting out soda from accidently having it go down the wrong tube. Gary patiently waits for his coughing spell to end. It takes a while.

"Mom said he inspected property or something but I don't really know what that means," he answered, still coughing and trying to dry his shirt off with his hands.

Taking a few deep breaths, calmed Gary down. There was nothing he could do about their missing father. He briefly daydreamed of enacting revenge on the kids behalf, all the things he could do to their father to try and set things right for Cody and Kyle. He broke off another beer from the plastic.

"Flip those steaks why don't ya, I'll go get some plates." He sips his beer and puts it down and heads inside.

Kyle grabs the tongs off the side of the grill and flips the possum patties. Cody continues to ingest the sweet sugary nectar of off brand soda. The door opens and Gary walks back outside holding a stack of paper plates and a bottle of ketchup. He passes out the plates to the brothers.

"Help yourselves."

Kyle grabs the tongs and places a few possum steaks on everyone's plate. They watch Gary cover half his plate in ketchup and follow his lead. The plates get mildly soft and flimsy after being soaked in so much ketchup.

"Forks?" Kyle asked, with his plate on his lap, the anticipation of trying his bounty rising.

"I'm outta clean ones. Just use your hands."

The three of them ate their steaks with their ketchup. Both the brothers enjoyed their meal. After dinner Gary sent them on their way before it got too dark. Kyle, with a big smile on his face, picked up his bike off the ground and waved to Gary with his whole arm. On the porch leaning against a railing, Gary waves back and he watches the two of them bike down the long driveway.

Chapter 6

Monday comes quickly and brings with it the routine of mourning the passing weekend and counting down the days till the next one. It was a busy morning of getting the piece of junk van started followed by the scheduled trapping of many vermin. After visiting several properties, he had collected a large amount of gophers and even a pesky possum. As busy as his schedule looked on paper, all the jobs were finished by lunch time. Like every lunch during the work week Gary headed to the convenience store.

The little bell sounds off as Gary enters the store, Margret looks up and greets Gary, then hunches back over the counter reading her newspaper. Gary smiles and waves and gathers his traditional lunch, a hot dog and a tall beer. He presents his items at the counter and then grabs a handful of lollipops from the jar to add to his purchases. Margret is still reading her newspaper, so focused on the article she doesn't yet notice Gary is ready to checkout. He waits for a few moments patiently, then decides to start eating his hot dog with all the fixings on it to see if she notices. Right in front of her he starts chowing down on the hot dog, some bits of relish fall on the counter. About half way through the hot dog he decides to open up his beer. At the sound of the fizzy snap of the tab breaking through the can she looks up and sees Gary drinking his beer in front of her.

"Oh my Gosh Mr. Bilson!" She laughed. Startled, she stood up straight and put the newspaper down. "How long have you been standing there? Long enough to almost have eaten your lunch I see. Sorry about that, I was reading about the possum bandit. He struck again over the weekend. Look." She turns the newspaper around and points to the article. "He did some sick things in that house. Hung up dead animals in this high school boy's bedroom during a party they were having. They think someone impersonated a pizza driver and that's how he got inside. They have the testimony of the real pizza driver who went there and he said some creepy fella dressed like him took the pizzas off of him and demanded he take his hat."

As she continued to ring up the lollipops one by one Gary stared at the article, reading intently. His adrenaline started pumping and he felt alive. He felt good. Maybe it was the article, maybe it was his new friendship with the brothers. He was in such a good mood he did something he has never had the courage to do before.

"Wow this is wild stuff." Rubbing his chin trying to act shocked.

"You know tonight I was going to sit at home alone and watch tv till I fell asleep, but I might be too scared to be by myself with this possum bandit still running around." He said facetiously with a smile. "How about we go out tonight for a drink?"

Margret, taken aback, started blushing as she totaled his items. She had the biggest smile and started to nervously tidy her hair, moving strands around behind her ears. "I would like that. but I'm not much of a bar gal. How about you come over tonight for dinner, let's say 6 o'clock?" Her voice cracked slightly.

"That sounds great!" He says excitedly as he hands her cash.

Margret smiles and writes her address on the back of Gary's receipt. "See you tonight Gary."

Gary folds it and puts it in his shirt pocket with some of his lollipops. As Gary picks up the rest of his items off the counter he asks, "May I take this?" Putting his finger on top of the newspaper.

"Oh yea sure no problem!" She nods and folds the paper up for Gary.

Before leaving, Gary pulls out a tube of lipstick in the shade Coral Blue No. 5. He takes the lid off and glides the semi gloss shade across both his lips, never breaking eye contact with Margret. He takes his napkin he had grabbed next to the hotdogs and kisses it, leaving a perfect impression of his lips on the napkin. He slides the napkin across the counter to her.

As he walks out of the convenience store he turns around and they give each other one more wave.

The whole drive back to his house he couldn't stop smiling. He rolled down the window to feel the breeze roll through his hair. He turned on the radio and cranked up the volume and started drumming with one hand against the steering wheel to the rock and roll while the other hand carried the beer. This was a rare moment of excitement and joy for Gary. He hadn't felt so alive in years. As he takes a large sip of his cold beer, suddenly a deer prances out of the bushes onto the road. With cat-like reflexes, Gary's foot darts from gas to brake. He drops his beer and his knuckles clenched white on the steering wheel. His beer is now spilling all over the floorboard. Despite his reaction time it wasn't enough. The van skids and slams right into the doe. Violently, it tumbles onto the front of the van, severely denting the hood before falling back to the street and taking the duct taped bumper down with it.

Whatever Gary's previous excitement level was right before the crash, it has now been replaced and doubled with anger. Without skipping a beat he swings the door open and kicks his beer can out onto the street with the side of his boot and hops out of the van. Standing before the deer his hands shake with fury and his breathing intensifies. He looks at the new damage done to the hood, looks back at the deer, and then at the bumper on the street. He bends down to pick up the tattered misshapen bumper and lifts it high above his head. With all his might he throws the bumper at the lying animal. He collapses back against the hood of his car and holds the bridge of his nose in utter frustration. Hoping a sucker will calm him down he takes a lollipop out of his pocket. His breathing now deep and focused, his teeth gritting the stick of the sucker. With a slow intensity he crouches down to hover over the deer.

He gently puts his hand on the doe's head. "Listen, you caught me in a good mood today so I'm not going to grab my ax in the back of my van and chop your filthy head off. I am starting to hate your kind more than possums. Congratulations, I didn't think that was possible. So I'll just let you rot here on the street and let nature have its way with you." Reaching back into his shirt pocket he pulls out another lollipop and unwraps it. With one hand he opens the mouth of the deer. With the other, he slides the sucker in and closes its mouth.

Once more, Gary examines the damage to his van. And once again he finds himself taping the bloodied bumper back on the vehicle. It takes quite a while and a lot of tape to get his bumper to stay on but eventually he manages to secure it high enough so it doesn't scrape the ground. He pops the hood and observes the large dent. He smashes the underside of the hood with a hammer attempting to knock the dents out. It's a very unsuccessful plan and it looks even more damaged and mangled than before. Groaning and muttering to himself he keeps trying. His arm grows tired and he gives up and shuts the hood and gives the deer one more angry glare and putters his way back home.

With a fresh can of cold beer from the fridge, and his newspaper article he sits down on his couch and begins to read the article about the possum bandit. He smiles and laughs at the testimonies and stories brought forward. Everyone was so wasted. Even Jake and the other girl he was with described the attacker as a giant man with a hairy face. He lets out a few chuckles of amusement as he reads the pizza drivers account of what happened. The driver did happen to describe Gary moderately accurately but it was dark out when they met, rendering his description of Gary vague and lacking.

Under the end table next to the couch he reaches down on the bottom shelf and pulls out a large book, some scissors, and tape. The black book had an old tattered cover with the edges fraying, and three pieces of decorative twine laced around the top bottom and middle of the spine. No markings or inscriptions on the front or back, just a fairly old thick scrapbook.

He opens the book up to the first page, faded yellow from time, centered on the page is a cut out newspaper article. His fingers glide down the newspaper article as he reads some of it. The article tells of a cafeteria worker at the local highschool who was serving lunch one day. And in one of the empty bowls she was filling with tomato soup she noticed something strange in the ladle. As the soup poured out of the ladle it revealed an unknown hairy and disgusting tiny head of an animal the report stated. Upon further inspection from authorities they identified the head in the soup as belonging to a possum. A full scale health inspection was done following this incident, and prior to that six additional possum heads were found in the vat of soup. The article stated there were no suspects as to who would do such a horrendous thing. Gary smiled as he read, chuckling to himself trying to imagine the horror on the lunch ladies face as she discovered the head. He had only wished a student found it in their bowl first.

Turning the page he chuckles once more at the title of the next article. *Dead possums found in melted snowman in front of police station.* He reminisces on when he built a snowman in the public park across from the police station. One night he set out to build the snowman and started each section of the snowman with a dead possum. As he rolled the possum in the snow the ball got bigger. As it got bigger, he stuffed and rolled more possums into it. When the snowman was finished in the park it was a beautiful addition. It complimented the Christmas lights in the trees surrounding. It was facing the police station and had a big smile made out of coal and a classic carrot nose. It greeted onlookers with holiday cheer with its little waving stick arms. When the temperature started to rise however, the snowman began shedding its frosty layers and unveiling its morbid core, the dead possums. They appeared through the snow as if eating the snowman from the inside out. When authorities cleaned up the mess, the final possum count found in the snowman was thirteen.

Several of these types of articles fill the scrapbook and each page is a road down memory lane for Gary. These articles go back many years and they have given many names to this terrorizer. Names like Possum Bandit, Roadkill Collector, Possum King, and many more. The kids in the area have their own urban legends circulating amongst themselves. Every local knows of the many incidents involving these creatures. No one however has been able to link these cruel and psychotic events to anyone.

He turns to an empty page and cuts out the tale of his most recent act. Carefully he centers it on an empty page and tapes the article on all sides into the book. He rubs his hand over the page like a precious gem, admiring his own work of torment. Gary closes the book and puts it back on the bottom shelf of the end table and quietly drinks his beer in silence, mentally attempting to build up his confidence for his date. When he first asked Margret out, he was riding on an emotional high seeing his work again published in the local paper. But now that his thoughts have settled, he has taken on somewhat of a nervous demeanor.

He finishes his beer and decides to start preparing for his date, starting with a hot shower.   Staring into a foggy mirror he wipes the surface with a hand towel, bringing clarity as he stares back at himself with his long wet black hair. He shaves his face clean like usual and runs his fingers through his wet hair, pondering how he could style it to look more dapper. Normally he just lets it dry and the hair figures itself out. But tonight was special. It was his first time going on a date since her disappearance. Unsure of what to do, he looks through the various bathroom products in the cabinet underneath the sink. He manages to find a bottle of hair gel. Gary opens the top and brings the bottle under his nose and smells the contents, not knowing how old or even where this bottle came from. Regardless of the unknowns, he applies a generous amount of gel to his hands and slicks his long black hair all the way back. Looking like a vampire that sells pre owned vehicles, Gary starts hunting for the perfect shirt to wear to dinner. He sifts through a few polos but decides polos aren't really date worthy clothes, but clothes for businessmen who lack nice shirts. Besides, he wouldn't want to wear anything resembling what he wore during the possuming at Jake's party.

The rest of his shirts are t-shirts. The only button down he can find is his tan shirt he wears to work so settles for that and puts it on. All the pants he can find in his room are old jeans and his one pair of dress pants he modified into shorts. He sorts through his jeans and chooses the least tattered and frayed pair and puts them on. He then notices his fingernails are getting pretty long and there is a lot of dirt stuck underneath them. Gary sits on his bed with his knife and starts carefully cutting away at his fingernails. Some pieces fall on the bed, some on the floor, some shoot off towards the wall as the knife breaks through each nail and launches it. He examines his fingers. Pleased with the results, he brings his foot up on the bed and begins cutting away at his toenails. One toenail makes a light tapping sound as it hits his dresser.

Gary's eyes follow it and he sees the turned down picture frame. He pauses, staring at the frame, then opens his top dresser drawer and hides the picture in it and closes it up.

After the self manicure Gary goes back to the bathroom mirror to make sure he looks presentable. Dressed in his work attire, the only real difference is his hair is slicked back and stiff. With a satisfied nod of approval he then goes into the kitchen and grabs a bottle of cleaning spray and mists the air in front of him and walks through it. Clean fingernails, fresh scent, and combed hair, Gary grabs another six pack out of his fridge and the receipt with Margret's address written down on it and struts out the door.

He turns the key and the engine coughs and whines, then sputters to silence. With more force he twists the key again, holding it tight and leaning into it the engine coughs again but it gets quieter even faster and goes silent. Overtaken by rage, with all his strength he turns the key with the flick of his wrist and he hears a loud clicking sound. The key snapped off in the ignition. Seething over the steering wheel he makes a tight fist and punches the steering wheel with a fury of blows. After a spree of punches he loses his breath, and during his fit of rage not a strand of his rock hard hair was out of place. However, the horn of the vehicle was now stuck and holding a long loud continuous blast. Gary tries hitting it a few more times but is unsuccessful in silencing his vehicle. Livid, he pushes the van door open and takes a few steps away from the van, then whips back around. With impressive speed he draws his pistol and without taking any real time to aim he starts firing at the steering wheel through the open door. He fires five shots. The first two hit the glove box on the passenger side. It swings open and a new crack erupts all the way through it. The other three shots hit the steering wheel and the horn quiets down.

A new level of self control has been reached. He didn't empty his entire clip into the van. He holsters his firearm and marches off towards the garage with his arms stiff and his shoulders hunched forward while muttering profanities under his breath. He crouches down and lifts the garage door over his head. His eyes scan the dusty boxes and piles of old junk before they settle on a yellow set of handlebars with black rubber grips. In order to reach the bike, Gary has to climb onto an old card table with stacks of dusty boxes on top and underneath it. He reaches over a tall stack of boxes and is able to grab a hold of the handlebars. He attempts to pull the bike out from the mound of junk but the bike just has too much clutter around it. He tries moving some boxes out of the way by throwing them across the garage. Their contents spill out onto more boxes. Despite his efforts the stubborn bike refuses to be let loose. Gary finds some rope lying around and ties it to the bike's handlebars. With the coiled rope, still standing on the table with the boxes, he tosses the rope up and over some rafters.

He grips the rope with both hands and starts pulling as hard as he can. The bike begins to shift and lift in the clutter. Gary jumps up, suspended now in the air he tries using his body weight to lodge the bike free. The bike slowly starts to breach the surface of the clutter as he slowly descends back down towards the table. All of a sudden the bike breaks free from whatever it was caught on. The bike flies into the air and Gary crashes down on the table with a loud crash. The table breaks beneath him and crumbles onto the boxes below. Gary tumbles and rolls off of the garage debris and crash lands into the driveway. Tangled in the rope, he wiggles free and stands up and attempts to brush off a new thick layer of dust on his pants and shirt, not a strand of his hair out of place. He grabs his bike from atop the junk pile and drags it out onto the driveway. He grabs the six pack and paper with Margret's address from the van.

Finally he is on his way to see Margret. Pedaling fast and sweating profusely he rides up and down the country roads not wanting to be any more late than he already is. One hand balances the beer on the grip and the other hand steadies the handlebars. He pedals past the deer he hit earlier. He smiles, amused at the lollipop still in its mouth. Down the main road he passes the convenience store. Further up the road he reaches a four way intersection. He turns right, about to cross the railroad tracks when the crossing lights flash and sound off the chimes that a train is inbound. The arms come down and block Gary's path. Exasperated Gary lets out an audible grumble and slouches back on his seat and waits for the train. It's not a quick passenger train like he hoped for, but an unbelievably long freight train. The first engine passes in front of Gary with its whistle blowing loudly. He turns and tucks his head into his shoulder trying to spare his hearing. He watches the graffitied train cars rumble by, entranced by the hypnotic sound of the clicking and clacking. Losing patience Gary looks for the end of the train but it's nowhere in sight. Just box car after box car after box car. Even some of the cars next to him and at the intersection turn off their vehicles anticipating a long wait. In frustration Gary plucks a beer from the plastic and hurls it right at the train. The beer explodes against the train car, a cloud of mist and foam erupts. Gary hears a honk from a car behind him. He turns around to see a woman scowling at Gary disapprovingly and a gentleman in the passenger seat that Gary assumes to be the husband, just laughing uncontrollably. Now even more agitated, Gary takes another beer from the six pack, maintaining eye contact with the rude woman in the car. He opens the beer and takes a drink. With a furious throw he chucks the beer directly towards the woman. With a loud thud it splashes beer all over the windshield. The woman's jaw dropped. She was in utter disbelief. As soon as the can of beer made contact with the windshield, the husband had opened up his door and was already getting out to confront Gary. Gary takes a third beer and snaps it from the plastic and hurls it high above the man's head. Like an old timey gunslinger Gary quickdraws his firearm and shoots the beer directly over his head. Beer rains down all over the man and in sheer terror he puts his hands up and walks backwards towards his vehicle. The woman's expression remains unchanged. At this time the crossing guards lift and Gary stands up on his bike and pedals to Margret's house.

Chapter 7

Gary glides on his bike down the street trying to match the house numbers to his piece of paper. After a few minutes of searching he finds a match. A little one story gray house with white trim and a red door. The lawn is small and there were colorful flowers planted next to the windows. He brings his bike to a halt and climbs off of it and walks it up the driveway between two cars. The car on the right he recognized from the convenient store Most likely Margret's, an ordinary red sedan in seemingly good shape. The car on the left was a different story. It reminded Gary of his van to some degree. Blue paint missing on the doors and the hood, thin wiry scratch marks above the rear tire and a big dent on the front bumper. Gary puts his beers on the hood of the blue car and tucks his bike between it and the garage door. With the flick of his foot he drops the kickstand and rests the bike down. He grabs the beer and starts walking to the front door. As he reaches the door, the kickstand starts to slide away from the bike, eventually it folds back up and the bike smashes against the blue car. Shattered glass rains down on the concrete as the bike handlebars impale the headlight. In a nervous panic Gary drops his beer and runs over to the bike, his boot crunching through the glass. He prys the bike from the headlight and rolls it around to the side of the house and leans it into some bushes. When he returns to the front door one of the beer cans he had dropped has sprayed all over the porch and door leaving a bubbly sticky mess. Too nervous to be mad he picks up the remaining two beers and starts squeegeeing the foamy beer off the porch with the bottom of his boot.

He takes a deep breath and nervously touches his hair making sure it's still looking nice and in place. A wet paste comes off on his fingers. The sweat from biking all the way into town has made his hair product runny. Thick beads of gel dangle from the roots of his hair streaking down his forehead. Rubbing his fingers clean on his shirt he rings the doorbell. With great anticipation and anxiety, the time he stands on the porch waiting for the door to open feels like an eternity. The door finally opens wide and Gary looks up to see Margret and her curly red hair and big eyes and a bigger smile greeting him. Margret's smile quickly turns sour and then concerned as she looks upon Gary and his condition. Creepily slicked back and melting hair, dirt and dust all over his sweat stained clothes, and the scent of beer emitting from all around.

"What happened to you?" She asks with a concerned look on her face.

Gary clears his throat and fumbles with the beer in his hands. "I had to bike over here."

"Car troubles?" She snapped back with curiosity.

"Yes ma'am, wouldn't start."

She tilts her head to the side and glances at the beer. She points to them and asks, "Did you drink the other four on the way here?"

On edge Gary rubs his cheek, "No ma'am, I fell on my bike and the beer scattered across the road, three of them broke open and were spraying everywhere and when I was walking to grab the fourth a truck ran over it."

Margret looked at Gary up and down, and burst out laughing and stepped aside to motion him in. "I don't mean to be rude, but that's hilarious! I hope you're ok."

Gary joined her laughing as he entered the home.

The smell of spices and the sounds of cooking overcame Gary's senses as he took off his boots. In the other room he could hear what sounded like water boiling and something sizzling on a pan. He followed Margret through the living room and into the kitchen. Mashed potatoes boiled in a big silver pot and several thin slices of chicken were sizzling on a large skillet. Margret flipped the chicken with some tongs.

"Alrighty let me give you the grand tour." She sets the tongs down and waves her hand to the side. "This is the kitchen, nothing fancy." Gary simply nods and follows her back towards the main room. "And this is the living room, and down that hall are some bedrooms and the first door on your left is a bathroom." She points down the hall as she walks back to the kitchen. "Dinner is almost ready if you want to grab a seat."

Gary shuffles over past the kitchen island towards the small square dinner table and pulls out one of the three chairs to sit in. Margret starts plating some of the food from the stovetop, and as she does a noise can be heard down the hallway. A door swivels open and little pattering paws can be heard running down the hallway. The claws of the little black poodle tap the kitchen tile as it turns the corner, its feet sliding out from underneath itself. The dog stops to face Gary and starts growling.

"Oh don't mind Sammy. She's all bark and, well I guess some bite too." Margret said, trying to comfort Gary, walking by the angry little dog to set the plates of food down. "You a dog person or a cat guy?" She asked, grabbing some drinks from the fridge.

"Neither." Gary said, refusing to back down and break eye contact with the little devil.

After some time Sammy stopped growling and approached Gary's chair. Gary assumed he had established his dominance so he reached down to pat the head of the poodle, but before his hand could even touch its mangie forehead, Sammy snapped at Gary's fingers drawing lots of blood.

"Son of a!" Gary shouted, lifting his shirt to reach for his gun. Quickly he realized what he was doing and pretended to scratch an itch on his side.

"Sammy! In the cage!" Margret shouted at the dog. The dog instantly tucked its stringy rat tail between its frail legs and hid away in his cage in the corner of the kitchen. Gary stood up and went to the kitchen sink and put his finger under some cold running water as Margret went down the hall to grab a bandaid.

"Here ya go Gary." She said feeling embarrassed. "I'm so sorry about that."

As Gary applied the band aid, footsteps could be heard coming from the hall.

"Sally! Come say hi before you take off to dance class." A young teenage girl with black athletic pants and a matching jacket, and curly red hair just like her mothers appeared from the hallway. Her face buried in her phone as she entered the kitchen.

"This is my daughter Sally. Sally, this is Gary." Margret announced cheerfully trying to put the dog bite behind them.

Sally looked up from her phone for a split second and mumbled something resembling a hello and her head sprang back to her phone. Immediately her face became distraught and she looked back up at Gary, and she became white as a ghost.

"Ok mom love you, gotta run." And Sally speedily walked out the door and drove off. Her car sounded almost as bad as Gary's van as it puttered past the house.

Gary was concerned and confused about the look Sally gave him. He sat back down at the table and Margret sat down next to him. "Teenagers." She sighed. Gary let out an uncomfortable chuckle as he began cutting the chicken.

"You have any kids Gary?" she asked, not entirely sure what were appropriate conversation topics for a first date.

Gary did not like personal questions. He was a very reserved soul but he mustered all his energy to answer because he did in fact fancy Margret.

"No." He said as he stared down at his plate and filled his mouth with chicken.

"Ever married?" she continued, trying to read Gary's body language on whether a lighter topic of discourse should be pursued.

His chewing slowed. Still staring at his plate, he swallowed his food and wiped his mouth with a napkin. Uncomfortably he starts gliding the prongs of his fork over the edge of the plate making an eerie screeching noise. Margret gives it a few moments and as she takes a sip of the beer Gary had brought, just as she opens her mouth to try and steer the conversation elsewhere, Gary starts clearing his throat.

"Yes." He exhaled heavily through his nose and scooped up some mashed potatoes.

Margret didn't know what to ask next. She felt as if she hit a soft spot and wanted to lighten the mood but feared that she had set the tone for the rest of the evening.

"She went missing a long time ago. She had some issues." He tapped on the side of his head still staring at his plate. "One night she just left, and no one has heard from her since."

They both sat there in silence, both aware that this first date was not going particularly well. Gary started to panic inside, aware of how gloomy things have been these last few minutes. His mind raced with various questions or comments he could say to try and save this date. In a panic he blurted out, "What's your favorite meat?" Instantly his face cringed at how lame that was. Margret's eyebrows raised. At first she seemed unimpressed, but as she thought of how the night began and is currently unfolding she couldn't help but laugh. Her laugh, once again contagious, got hold of Gary as their spirits lifted a little.

"I like chicken, and how about we start over. I'll pretend you didn't show up to my house all dirty and smelling like beer, and you pretend I asked you a softball question like, what kind of movies do you like?" Both of them smile as they enter into a more positive mindset together, only to be interrupted by a vibrating cell phone on the countertop. "That can wait." She smiled. The phone finally stopped vibrating only to begin again. Margret rolls her eyes and lets out an exasperated sigh as she gets up to check it.

"Hi Sally. How…." She quickly went from annoyed to deeply concerned, her voice now stressed. "Ok I'm on my way." Her hands trembling, she started scrambling for her keys.

"Everything alright?" Gary asked, convinced that something terrible had happened.

"Margret has been in an accident. I have to go." She bolted out the door and sped off in a hurry, the dog rushing to the door and barking behind her. Gary, left alone in this woman's house, is not sure what to do with himself. He's not sure if he should leave, or clean up, or stay till she gets back. He sat there for a moment trying to decide what to do, and then continued eating his dinner. She probably wouldn't want it to go to waste, he thought to himself. Sammy the dog sits down next to him hoping Gary would give him some chicken. "Now you like me?" Gary sneered at the dog. He polished off the rest of his beer and started working on Margret's. "It should have been you in that accident." Gary said to Sammy, still mad about the bite. Gary ended up eating all of Margret's dinner as well, the bike ride made him extra hungry. Now full of two home cooked meals and a couple of beers, Gary got up in search of the bathroom.

As he empties his bladder he looks over at the shower curtain, intrigued by the patterns and intricate shapes that made up its design. All of a sudden it clicked. He remembered his time at Jake's party hiding in the tub as a red headed girl clenched the side of the tub vomiting. It was Sally. Gary's face went white as a sheet as he zipped up and fell back against the wall with his hands on his head. His heart beating fast and his mind racing, he dashed towards the kitchen and desperately rummaged through the fridge in search of some cold liquid comfort. He found another beer and with great haste opened it and began drinking.

It took some time but Gary eventually calmed down some. He figured that Margret probably wouldn't have allowed Sally to go to such a wild party, so at least he had some leverage over her. But the question remained, how and when did she spot Gary? He continued to drink his new beer and ponder what he could do in order to ensure Sally didn't rat him out as the infamous local possum bandit. Inciting fear by intimidation was the best he could come up with to try and keep Sally quiet. It wasn't a great plan, but most of Gary's plans were not exactly thought out. He walked down the hall, examining the photos on the wall trying to extract any sort of clues that he could build into a plan. The photos were mostly of Margret and Sally. There were a couple of pictures of the dog but none of the father.

He comes across the first door on the right and twists the doorknob to peer in. The room had light purple walls with white trim, and several posters of teen pop star sensations covering the wall. It was easy to figure out that this was Sally's room. It was very neat and tidy. Gary walked around to the bed and started snooping around the dresser. A few nic-nacs and trinkets sat atop the dresser but nothing Gary could make use of. Next he began digging through her dresser drawers, pulling out all the folded clothes looking for any secrets she might be hiding. At the bottom of the top drawer he found a small leather bound book with a silver latch on it. His pencil-like fingers snatched the book up. He flipped the silver clasp open and gazed at the pages of Sally's diary. Excited to dig into the diary more later, he placed it in his back pocket to take home. He put the folded clothes back into the dresser trying to make it look the way it did before he rummaged through it. After his best attempt at covering his tracks he slipped out of the room and closed the door.

As he was leaving the house about halfway down the hall his curiosity got the best of him and he turned back around in search of Margret's room. He opened another door to find a queen size bed with an end table and some books on it. There were no decorations on the wall, it was a fairly plain room. He walked over to the end table and looked over the books. They were all cheesy romance novels, the kind you find at supermarkets near the checkstands. He scoffed, picking up one of the books to give it a once over. He put it back down and noticed a picture frame face down on the table. At that moment he stopped breathing but he didn't realize it. He let out a big breath as he snapped out of the trance. He didn't dare turn over the picture. He just couldn't.

As he bent down to put on his boots he heard a loud crunching noise coming from the kitchen. He leaned to the side to see what it was. He saw Sammy eating dry food out of his little red dog dish. Gary noticed a tennis ball a few steps from him, so he walked over to it and kicked it down the hall. With food still in the dog's mouth, he ran towards the noise and scurried down the hall after the ball. His heavy boots thunder over the kitchen tile with each step as he approaches the dog dish. He picks the bowl up and takes a few moments to find the trash can under the sink. The dog returns with the ball and drops it at his feet and notices Gary is holding the food dish. Its little black rat tail was wagging with joy, excited to chase the ball and or eat some more food. Both those dreams were crushed as Gary pulls the trash can out from under the sink and slowly pours Sammy's dinner into it. On Gary's way out the door he picks up the tennis ball and pretends to throw it down the hall. Sammy runs half way down the hall then turns around, not sure where the ball went. Gary walks out the front door and chucks the tennis ball over a neighbor's fence. He feels around his pockets and grabs a lollipop and pops it in his mouth as he lifts his bike off of the broken glass from the headlight incident and pedals home, but not before checking Margret's mail box. It was empty.

Eager to dive into Sally's diary, Gary struts straight to his couch, bypassing the beer in the fridge. He brings out the little book from his back pocket and falls back on the couch and starts flipping through the pages. In the midst of his snooping, he leans over towards the end table and opens the drawer and pulls out a blue pen. Every name that Sally mentions in her diary Gary circles aggressively, and she mentions quite a few people. Friends, crushes, teachers she likes and hates, kids in her dance class, all sorts of people she interacted with were littered throughout her writings. And to Gary, they were potential targets. He began imagining all the different things he could do to strike fear into his new subjects. How dare Sally recognize him.

Gutting and chopping up a possum and then stuffing it into her highschool crush's exhaust pipe with a tent pole crossed Gary's mind as he skimmed the pages. Maybe he could tie some fishing line to a dead possum's little legs and make a puppet, then he could make a video of it dancing to some music and then smash it with a hammer. He could find all her dance class mates and put the dvd in their mailboxes. Perhaps he could clog the gutters of her teacher's homes with possums. It would be a more long term investment that would not provide immediate satisfaction until the rain season starts, but perhaps spacing out his terror would be more beneficial.

Gary was on the last written page of the diary and tucked in the crease of the page he found a folded up newspaper article. With great care, he unfolded it with anticipation. In his hands was the article about the possum bandit who struck at Jake's house party, that mentions the lead suspect was the mysterious pizza deliverer imposter. Gary leaned forward on the couch, his senses heightened, his adrenaline started pumping. He began reading her journal entry to discover she did in fact take notice of the pizza guy at the party. She and her friends noticed him when he first arrived and they couldn't stop laughing at his short shorts. His general appearance according to the diary was very memorable, with his greasy long hair and skinny frame with the cut off dress pants turned into shorts. She wrote how the pizza guy was the running joke between her friends that evening. Sally mentions how when her friends were taking shots at the party, they called them shorts. Admittedly she writes it's not very funny, but in the moment it was absolutely hilarious. She continues writing that she noticed him go upstairs but doesn't remember seeing him come down. The diary mentions that if that was in fact the legendary possum bandit, then the party would be something the kids at school would consider a monumental event in their towns history. Stories would be passed down for ages about the party, and she could say she saw the suspected possum bandit with her own eyes. Sally admits in her writing that she doesn't remember much of the events from later in the evening, as she was drinking a bit too much and only remembers fuzzy snapshots of the night from a certain point. One of those snapshots included a monster in the bathtub, a demon hovering over her and her friend as they vomited in the tub.

Gary sat there for a few moments, almost dumbfounded at the coincidence that the person he was interested in dating, had a daughter that now knew who he was and his secrets. How could he be so careless? Was he careless, or was it just bad luck? He couldn't help but think that maybe it was just a matter of time before he was recognized.

Now filled with even more anxiety and fear, Gary rips out the last dated page in the diary and crosses out the word 'bandit' in Sally's entry and replaces it with 'KING'. Gary nervously smiled. He felt a bit more in control with his edit, and didn't agree with the use of the word bandit. He wasn't exactly stealing possums after all. After reading the journal he grabs his own scrapbook with his own newspaper articles and turns to the last page. In the drawer of the end table he pulls out some glue and transplants her diary entry into his scrapbook. Another trophy, maybe the most important one.

He sat there a few moments waiting for the glue to dry, once it did he put the scrapbook and diary on the end table. Still dirty and smelling like beer he decided he needed to shower and get a good night's sleep. He had work to do.

Chapter 8

The dark clouds stretched out over the sky blocking the morning sun rays as Gary marched through his property. With only an empty backpack, his usual everyday carry items, and his frantic thoughts, he made his way to the multiple possum traps near the thick brush. Gary had never been identified before in the history of his mischief. He pondered what he might be charged with if the police were involved. All he ever did after all, was relocate a few dead possums in unusual places and occasionally steal people's mail. Would this plan of inciting fear and intimidation into the witness by targeting her peers be the best route? Would she get the message and keep her mouth shut or turn me in? Gary mulled over these thoughts as they rang through his head like a bell. Does a darker path need to be taken? At this thought Gary stops in the woods and wipes his face with his hand and pulls out some lollipops from his shirt pocket and quickly throws them on the ground. His hands shaking, he pulls out a lighter and a stowed away cigarette and revisits his old habit.

He takes a long slow inhale and as he gazes up towards the gray sky through the trees. He exhales and watches the smoke dance in front of him. In a temporary trance he just stands there watching it curl and wave into nothing. The whole world was gray to him at this moment. The tall green trees, the small dark bushes and yellow flowers seemed dull and lifeless to Gary. The emotional high he had from an authentic human connection the night before was rapidly being replaced by the emptiness and fear he was all too familiar with.

His trance was interrupted by a noise, a twig cracking in the distance. His eyes focus on where he hears the noise from and what he sees next Gary can't explain. With wide eyes, a rush of adrenaline pumps through his veins as he sneaks closer to the creature that stands before him. It looks like a deer but something was different about it. It looks deformed, and when Gary got close enough to see it more clearly his jaw slacks and his cigarette falls to his feet. It is in fact a deer, but it is covered in a black ash, faint orange and red glowing cracks spider throughout the animal's charred skin. It was smoldering and giving off smoke. Gary could smell the burning flesh. Gripped with fear he draws his pistol and points it towards the sky and lets off a warning round hoping to either wake up from this dream or scare the animal away. The blacked doe's head swivels unnaturally fast towards Gary. Unphased, its large lifeless eyes gaze into his. Holding his breath he slowly brings the pistol down with the barrel pointed right at the creature. Little beads of sweat fall from his hairline as he stares down the barrel of his pistol at the deer, or whatever this thing was. Slowly Gary applies pressure to the trigger, his heart beating fast, the sweat now falling into his eyes. The trigger snaps and another round flies. The bullet impacts the deer right in the head. The top right half of its head explodes into ash, black dust and hundreds of bright glowing embers twinkle and hover in a cloud around the deer. One gray eye still looks back at Gary from its mangled head. The deer remains completely still.

Every second Gary grew more afraid and angry as the smoldering animal watched him. In a moment of panic and fear Gary takes a step toward the deer, stomping his foot down with a yell in hopes of scaring it away. His boot snaps a branch in half and the crack startles him and he leaps and stumbles forward. The hooves of the animal crunch the leaves on the ground as it takes a few gentle steps towards Gary. Each hoof burns into the forest debris as smoke trickles up from each step. Adrenaline pumps through Gary's veins as he now slowly starts to retreat, but the deer advances on Gary at an equal pace. A loud crack of thunder and a flash of lighting burst through the tree limbs. Gary jumps with a fright and heads off back towards the house in a full sprint, occasionally looking over his shoulder as the half headed deer pursues him at full speed. Heavy drops of rain begin falling and the dirt turns to mud, and in a matter of seconds Gary is sopping wet, his clothes heavy as he continues to run. He looks over his shoulder again and sees the deer still approaching but with each drop of rain that makes contact with the creature's ashy coat it causes a small ploom of smoke and ash to rise with a subtle sizzling and popping sound. He notices the creature getting smaller as the rain continues to assault it. Exhausted, out of breath, Gary stops and faces the sprinting deer and once again raises his firearm. Before he has a chance to pull the trigger, the deer is already in front of him, then it is running through him. A thick cloud of dark smog and embers pummel Gary. He lifts his hands to shield his face, closing his eyes tight. He slowly opens his eyes and peeks past his hands. The deer was gone. Only the sound of heavy rain pattering on the trees and dirt can be heard.

With shaky hands and unsettled nerves he unwraps another lollipop and teeths on it like a child attempting to calm down. He rubs his eyes and looks all around him and tries to wake up, but he isn't dreaming. A few moments go by before he regains enough courage to continue his way to the possum traps at the edge of the brushy hill. His eyes dart around the forest as he marches on, looking for any more strange phenomenon, trying to contemplate what he just experienced. As Gary moved closer to the traps he heard faint hissing, cackling, and growling. The sounds blurred together like the roars of a crowd at a sports stadium as he drew closer to the base of the hill. He reaches the hill and upon seeing the traps, his jaw drops and his sweet treat falls out of his mouth and into the dirt. Possums were everywhere. The several cages in range of sight were packed to the brim with possums, their fur pressing through the wire of the cages hissing angrily. Around the cages where more possums circling they're trapped brethren, making urgent high pitched whining sounds. There had to be nearly fifty possums Gary thought to himself. He pondered how he would be able to exterminate them all. If only he had a gatling gun.

He approaches the nearest cage in front of him and looms over the trapped critters, the possums ignoring his presence as they screech and squirm around the cage. With a smooth draw and no hesitation, Gary fires off his entire clip, putting one bullet through one possum at a time with lightning fast speed and accuracy. The blasts of the gun shots sends the free roaming possums in a retreat and the thick brush behind the cages welcomes them to safety. Gary quickly fills his backpack with eight fresh kills from a single cage and forgets about the rest of the rodent filled traps for now. This has been a strange evening.

With a swift pace he backtracks through the woods to his home to the sound of low rumbles of thunder and the popping of raindrops against his shoulders. He gets to the run-down shed and unlocks the padlock. The rusty hinges screech as he forces the stubborn door open. A foul, almost visible smell rushes past Gary. It doesn't bother him at all. He fumbles towards the center of the dim shed bumping into various obstacles in the dark. Finally he feels the dangling beaded lightswitch and gives it a tug. Light pours forth from the bulb illuminating what most would consider a most unsettling sight. Mounted shelves covered the walls with cages of mostly dead decaying possums. A few were still alive, eating their fallen comrades to satisfy the hunger. Mounted possum heads filled the spaces between the shelves, and poorly taxidermied possums lay about a metal table with rusty tools spread about. There were even possums hanging from the rafters above by rope and string, dripping with a black thick goo. A metal garbage can was placed in the corner of the shed and was filled to the top with a half and half blend of gophers and possums.

Clearing the metal table off with the swipe of his arm Gary empties the contents of his backpack. The dead possums slump out onto the table and Gary stacks them in a pile. He proceeds to take one of the rodents from the pile and holds it up by the back of the neck. A little tongue dangles out of its mouth as Gary maneuvers its legs in what vaguely resembles a dancing like motion. He hums to himself and bobs his head back and forth to the rhythm of the dancing possum. He chuckles to himself as he bends down underneath the table and reaches for a damp and sticky blood stained cardboard box. He rests it on the table and sifts through various junk until eventually he pulls out a few short metal rods and some string. He lashes the two rods together to form an X shape, then proceeds to tie one piece of string on each end of the rusty pipes. He then ties the strings to each leg of the possum. Lifting the metal rod above the table the possum unevenly and disturbingly dangles from the twine. Gary starts rotating and bobbing the rods to make his new puppet dance and move to his will. Greatly amused, Gary puts the puppet down and rushes out of the shed and returns with a portable radio and a flashlight. He tunes the radio to a modern pop station playing an upbeat song with a constant bass drum and proceeds to play with the puppet using the flashlight as a spotlight.

After the recital was over Gary put a little duct tape name tag on the puppet that reads 'Sally'. He places the finished puppet on an old fifty-five gallon drum and starts on the next possum to puppet transformation. As he ties the string around the first leg of the possum his stomach lets out a hungry growl. Placing his hand on his stomach he walks out of the shed and into his kitchen in search of some food. His wet boots leave a path of mud behind him. He glances at the clock as he opens his pantry. A look of surprise dawns his face, not expecting it to be so late in the evening. He shuffles through some items until he finds a jar of peanut butter. Twisting off the lid and like a grizzly bear he dips his narrow paws into the jar and scoops out a big clump of peanut butter, suckling it off his fingers.

Without any water or beverage to help it go down Gary starts coughing wildly and uncontrollably and thick drops of spit and peanut butter hurl back into the open pantry. In the midst of his coughing fit there's a knock at the door. In the middle of hacking up peanut butter, Gary opens the front door. Cody and Kyle cover their faces with their hands shielding them from the barrage of peanut butter spray launching from Gary's mouth.

Eventually Gary regains his composure.

"What are y'all doing here?" He asks the boys wiping his mouth off with his arm.

"Our mom told us to go outside and play with friends." Kyle said, smiling with his thumbs nestled in the straps of his backpack.

Gary starts sucking up the peanut butter on his arm that he just wiped from his mouth.

"Friends?" He said drying his arm off with his shirt.

"We brought our video games. We want to show you the new one we got!" Kyle said with great excitement, twisting his torso to show Gary the backpack.

Gary lets out a sigh.

"Well I was just in the middle of figuring out dinner. Have y'all eaten yet?" Gary said with mild exasperation, not having the heart to turn these youngsters away.

"We like pizza." Cody said deadpan.

Gary waited for there to be more to that sentence but there wasn't.

"Ok I guess I'll order a pizza…" He said, taking a step back to open the door for Cody and Kyle.

The two kids rush in and instantly plop down on the floor next to the television. In great haste they unload the backpack and start plugging in wires to set up the video game console. Gary shuts the door and heads to the kitchen to order some pizza from *Bottom Feeders*. After he orders a few pies he hangs up the old corded phone and sits on the couch. He looks out of the window at the orange and purple sky. The clouds and rain seem to have passed by for now and like a curtain parting, have revealed quite a magnificent sunset.

"Got it!" Cody said as the screen lights up with flashing colors and sounds.

"Woohoo!" Kyle says as he raises his fists with glee.

Gary, slouched on the couch, rolls his eyes and gets up to grab a beer from the fridge. Just as the fizz could be heard bubbling from the freshly opened cold bottle, there's another knock at the door. With another heavy sigh he forcefully places the beer on the table with gritted teeth and goes to open the door.

He opens the door and lets out an agitated, "Yes?"

His annoyed demeanor turns into embarrassment, surprised to see Margret.

"Hi Gary." She says with a soft smile.

"...Hi...What are you doing here?" Gary replies looking perplexed.

"Our date night kinda got interrupted and I wanted to surprise you and maybe cook up some dinner for us." She says while shuffling her feet looking bashful.

Gary hesitates for a moment. "Um...ya I mean."

"If you're busy I get it. I know it's kinda spur of the moment." She interrupts apologetically.

"No no no no," Gary says, opening the door a little more. "We can hang out tonight. I just ordered a pizza so you're off the hook for cooking." He smiles, and motions her to come in.

"How did you know where I live anyway?" He asked, trying to remember if he ever told her.

"Your Gopher van isn't very subtle. I've seen it parked here for years when I drive down this road." She laughed as she walked into the house.

She instantly notices the two boys sitting on the floor, their eyes glued to the TV.

"Oh, I didn't realize you had…" She paused for Gary to fill her in.

"Nephews." He said, loud enough for Cody and Kyle to look over at him. "These are my nephews, Cody and Kyle." He glared at the boys with an intense stare that demanded compliance. The boys looked at Margret and simply waved and turned back to their video game without saying a word.

Gary walks Margaret to the kitchen to grab her a drink.

"How's Sally doing anyway?" He asks as he sits down at the table, sliding an open can of beer towards her.

"Oh she's fine, a couple of scrapes and bruises, a broken arm and rib, and a concussion." She said trying to stay positive.

"I'm sure she will be fine. Kids are like geckos, or whatever lizard things that do that tail stuff." Gary said, stumbling over his words trying to comfort Margret.

She furrowed her eyebrows in confusion. "What?" She says tilting her head to the side.

"You know, you cut the tail off a gecko and it grows back, kids heal good... I guess that's my point." Gary said, now beginning to perspire. Margret could see his attempt at providing encouragement, even if it was a strange comment. She just giggled and smiled. After a short awkward pause Gary asks, "Do you want a snack or something while we wait for the pizza?".

"Sure!" Margret said with enthusiasm. "What ya got?"

Gary tapped his finger on the table as he searched his mind for a good snack idea.

"I have some peanut butter." He said sheepishly, nervously rubbing his eyebrow.

Margret gave him a curious look, with an unsure smile she nodded her head in approval.

"..Ya, ok, interesting appetizer but I like it." She chuckled as Gary grabbed two spoons and a jar of peanut butter.

"Cover your face!" Kyle shouted from the other room.

"Shut your filthy mouth!" Gary barked back without skipping a beat. His face now red as he sits back down at the table.

"Sorry about that, kids say some weird stuff sometimes." He said as he opened the jar.

"No we don't!" Kyle shouted back over the sounds of the loud video game. "He coughed peanut butter all over our faces!"

Gary leaned on the table towards Margret with his elbow anchored to the table and he pointed towards the living room. "They are lying, I don't spit peanut butter on kids." He said in a strained whisper, trying to not be heard by the kids.

"Yes you do!" Cody shouted joining the conversation.

Gary's lips tighten together and his breathing becomes heavy. Margret bursts out laughing, "You guys are too funny!"

Gary regains his composure and calms down and the two of them start digging into the peanut butter together. As a joke, Margret shields her face with her hands as Gary licks some peanut butter off the spoon. They each got a kick out of it, and when Gary started choking on the peanut butter during his laughter, Margret had to cover her mouth to keep her peanut butter in as well. Gary hacks and spits peanut butter all over the table, and once Margret finishes eating her bite, she explodes into uncontrollable laughter.

Gary grabs some paper towels and starts wiping up the mess. Margret, winding down from her laughter, says, "So I didn't know you had siblings." Trying to start up a conversation as she watches an embarrassed Gary cleaning up his spit.

"Uhhhh." Gary says and stops wiping for a moment. "Oh yea siblings." He said connecting the dots that if he has nephews, they have to come from family. "Ya they are my brother's kids, well, I mean he didn't...you know." Gary scrubs the spit and peanut butter even harder. "He got his wife pregnant...and the...those kids in the living room um...they came out of her so...so ya they're my brother's kids with the help of their mom." Now extremely uncomfortable in his lying, Gary wipes the sweat beading up on his forehead off with his peanut butter covered paper towel and a thick brown smudge of peanut butter spread across his forehead.

"You have um…" Margret looks at Gary and waves her finger in front of her forehead. Gary swipes some peanut butter off and looks at his fingers and starts swearing profanities under his breath.

"I'll be right back." He stands up red in the face and cleans himself up in the bathroom.

Margret gets up and wanders around the kitchen while she waits. Taking little peeks into cupboards, curiously exploring a single man's kitchen. She makes her way around to the fridge and sees generic alphabet magnets scattered across the fridge door. Two names were spelled out with the magnets, Hunter and Claire. The H, U, N, and T magnets were holding up the note with the coordinates.

After thoroughly exploring the kitchen, Margret migrates with her beer into the living room and sits on the couch and sets her drink on the end table. As the kids keep quiet and focus on their game Margret sits there and looks around at the decorations, or lack thereof. Her eyes scan for any pictures of Gary or his friends and family but there were none on display.

With a peanut butter free face Gary returns from the bathroom. He finds Margaret in the living room and goes to sit on the other side of the couch. Unsure of what to say he grabs a lollipop out of his pocket and offers it to Margret. She leans forward and takes the lollipop from his hand.

"You and your lollipops." She says with a mild chuckle.

Gary simply nods and takes one out of another pocket for himself to enjoy. Kyle looks over toward the sounds of the lollipops being unwrapped and asks Gary, "Can I have one?"

With the sucker in his mouth, Gary stares at Kyle in the eyes for a few seconds before replying with an annoyed, "No."

Kyle scowls at Gary and hunches back over his video game controller and keeps playing. A few attempts of small talk are made between Gary and Margret but many minutes are spent in an awkward silence as they drink their beer and suck on the lollipops and watch the kids play.

The silence is interrupted by a knock on the door.

"Pizza!" The kids yell in unison.

Gary pushes himself up off the couch and opens the door. Gary's jaw suddenly drops and shifts as his eyes lock with the chubby pizza guy with the angelic blonde hair. He looks over his shoulder and takes a step out the door and closes it behind him. He looks down at the pizzas in his hands, then back up at the delivery driver who is just as shocked as Gary.

"I can just go, pizza's on me." He said with a tremble in his voice, trying to hand the pizzas over.

Gary continued to gaze, trying to figure out his next move. This guy now knew where Gary lived, and he was the person that took his hat and pizzas and is labeled as the prime suspect in the possum crimes. He could only assume the pizza man had connected the dots. Gary holds up his index finger and mouths the word, "wait." He cracks the door open behind him.

"There is a problem with the order. I'm returning the pizzas and speaking with his manager." He said, glancing back at the pizza guy making sure he stays put.

"Uh, what's wrong with the pizza?" Margret replied. " Is there a dead rat in it?" She laughed to herself.

"No…" Gary yelled back, looking up at the door frame trying to conjure his next lie. "They shaped the pepperonis into an inappropriate shape. It's unacceptable." And he slams the door and points towards his van and walks towards the pizza guy aggressively forcing him to back up. He opens the back of his van and drags the kid inside by his shirt collar, the pizzas falling on the ground. Gary ties him up with tape, ropes, and bungee cords. The pizza man's fear was heightened by what he saw in the van, a shotgun, rusty tools and buckets of small animals, the pungent odor bringing more tears to his eyes. Unable to speak, he just lays on the floor of the van shaking. Gary slams the door shut and grabs the pizzas and heads to the red truck with the illuminated pizza sign *Bottom Feeders* on top and drives the vehicle behind his house into the woods.

Chapter 9

She sips on her beer, waiting for Gary to return with the pizzas. Her thumb unknowingly wipes away the droplets of condensation on the cold bottle as she ponders what could be so terribly wrong with a pizza order that he needed to go into town to sort out. Her gaze wanders around the room, trying to discover tidbits about who Gary was in the details of his home. The unfolded blankets on the chairs, the peeling outdated wallpaper, the small crumbs that rocketed up out of the carpet as her foot slid over the shag fibers, she concluded that tidiness and general cleanliness were not something Gary valued.

Her gaze migrates over to where she was about to instinctively set down her beer, the coffee table. Two books sat on the table, a small leather bound book with a silver latch on top of a larger and thicker scrapbook. Without hesitation Margret swapped the beer for the small book, she started to unlock the latch but then stopped. The sudden thought that this could and probably was some sort of diary popped in her head, and she set it back down not wanting to invade Gary's privacy. The scrapbook however, did not have a latch on it. So she just figured that it would be okay to peruse.

She places the big book on her lap and runs her fingers over it. With great anticipation, hoping to see a scrapbook filled with some of Gary's closest friends and family, she opens the book to the first page. The old newspaper article greeted her with mild disappointment and concern. She skimmed over the article about a possum head being found in the soup at the local school. She shook her head in disgust, even though it happened years ago she remembered that day as if it were yesterday. She remembers having had to make up an excuse to her little girl why she wouldn't be getting money to buy lunches at school any more.

She turns the page hoping for a happier newspaper clipping, but finds herself reading another report of the known possum bandit. Why? She thought to herself as she flipped through story after story, newspaper clipping after another of the gruesome events of the local possum bandit. Now on the last page, she found a smaller page, handwritten and glued in the book. As she read it she began to break into a cold sweat, as the author of the page paints a description that matches Gary and links him to the most recent possum event at the infamous party. She flips back a page to find the most recent article being that of the party incident. She reads the article fully and intently, then rereads the journal entry. On her second read through of the journal entry, she noticed something that made her stomach drop to the floor. She recognized the handwriting to be her daughters.

With shaky hands she immediately closes the book and sets it back on the table and grabs the diary. This time without hesitation she opens the silver latch and flips through a few pages and confirms her suspicion that this is in fact her daughter's diary. And after the last entry, a ripped out page.

She looks up from the journal towards the kids on the floor.

"What do you and your uncle like to do together?" She said, her nervous fingernails digging into the couch's armrest.

"Huh?" Kyle said, forgetting what Gary had said about them being his nephews.

"Gary...your uncle." She said, having to clear her throat.

"Oh yea, um, we just hang out…he taught me how to shoot a gun."

Margret sprung out of her chair. She knew something was wrong and needed to find out more. Cautiously, she walked down the hallway and peered in though the opening of the cracked door of Gary's bedroom. Blankets balled up on the bed and clothes on the ground, she tiptoed her way through looking for anything suspicious. A hat in the corner of the room caught her attention. Margret picks it up and sees the local favorite pizza restaurant's logo on the hat, *Bottom Feeders*. She unknowingly had not taken a breath since entering the bedroom, and released a violent exhale. As she did, tears of panic began swelling in the corners of her eyes. She wipes her eyes with the sleeve of her shirt trying to maintain composure. She walks towards the dresser and sees something through the crack of the top drawer of the partially closed dresser. She opens the drawer and sees a turned over picture frame. Being overloaded with her discoveries she begins to tear up even more at the thought of turning the frame over. With a deep breath and a slow exhale she mustered the courage to flip the frame over, and to her relief it was not more damning evidence pulling back the curtain of who Gary truly is.

The house they stood in front of looked brighter, like a fresh coat of paint was drying. Gary looked brighter, a genuine smile that stretched for miles, his arms wrapped around what Margret could only assume was his wife at the time. She was surprisingly pretty, way out of Gary's league she thought to herself. She had wavy brown hair and blue eyes and a smile even larger than Gary's. And she had one hand placed on her slightly billowing tummy. The happiness captured in this photo was contagious, and for a brief moment Margret's state of panic was gone and replaced with peace. Her state of peace was interrupted by the howling of the kids, cheering victoriously at whatever game they were consumed by. Putting the picture back down she went outside to the backyard to get some fresh air to try and clear her head. She surveyed the area looking for more clues. She was fairly convinced he was the possum bandit, but still a part of her couldn't accept it.

The red run-down shed stood in front of her, the dusk colored sky breaking through some of the natural separations in the warped wood. Deep down she knew that whatever evidence she was looking for would be found there. Having to talk herself into taking a look, she jogs over and pulls on the door. The clanging sound of the lock and door rattles through her arm. Helpless, she turned the dial a few times hoping luck was on her side, but it was a dead end. She walked around the side of the shed and held her eye up to some of the spaces in the wall to try and see inside, but there just wasn't enough light. She pounded on the wall and hung her head in defeat.

With a jolt of energy she sprang up and ran into the kitchen. She yanked the note with the numbers from underneath the magnets, the plastic letters scattered on the floor. Dashing back to the shed she starts spinning the dial hoping the numbers on the page were the code. After the third number she pulled down and the lock clicked open. The door is stiff and requires her whole body weight to drag the door open. The rusty screech of the hinges pierce her ears like nails on a chalkboard. A thick warm odor infiltrates her nostrils and she starts to gag uncontrollably trying not to vomit. Having to plug her nose she shuffles into the shed, the floor boards creaking in the dark, her feet nudging various metallic sounding objects. She squints her eyes trying to adjust to the dark while looking for a light switch. Her hands flail in front and over her trying to feel for a drawstring or a chain. One of her hands feels a hard surface, and she uses it as her guide. She follows the surface with one hand and still waving her other to find a light switch. The hand on the hard surface encounters a soft, wet, fuzzy feeling object. She reflexively pulls her hand away in disgust and continues forward. Finally her waving hand slaps the beaded light switch and against her better judgment, she gives it a tug to illuminate her surroundings.

As a knee jerk reaction she covers her mouth with both hands, her head shrinks into her shoulders as she holds her breath to keep from screaming. She couldn't believe what she was seeing. Possums, mostly dead in cages, the few living ones moved slowly holding on for their small rodent life, but death was coming for them as well. Little heads mounted on the rafters, buckets and trash cans full of corpses, a bloodstained table full of junk, tools, a backpack and more creatures.

Margret looks down at the table and sees the dead possum her hand ran across. She looks at her bloody hand and gasps. She lifts up the backpack and finds the mask made of stitched together possum pelts. She has no idea what she is looking at but it is disturbing nonetheless. Just as she is about to flee the shed she notices the corpses in front of her are attached to wood pieces by string. Curiously she lifts up one of the corpses by the wooden pieces and the small animal body raised from it's slumber, slowly dancing for Margret as her hand began to tremble in complete terror. The light reflects off of the piece of duct tape on the puppet as it sways back and forth as if hung from the gallows. She notices there is something written on the tape. She leans in to inspect it and sees her daughter's name. With an ear shattering screech she throws the puppet as hard as she can against the cages on the wall and she runs out of the shed.

Gary is in the stolen truck in the woods behind his house, sucking on another lollipop. Killing time to make it seem like he actually went into town to sort out his pizza troubles before going back inside his home. With his head cocked back against the headrest, his eyes closed as he tries to think his way out of this. He had a pizza delivery driver tied up in the back of his van, he's hiding his truck in the trees of his backyard, and there is no way to make the pizza man unsee Gary. No legal way that is. There were too many frayed ends. His secret was unraveling. Sally, having an inkling of his mischievous behavior is bad enough. Now there's another witness tied up in the work vehicle. Gary thought of the unthinkable, murder. Maybe hide the bodies somewhere, or eat him, but he knew deep down he couldn't go through with it, and he knew he wasn't clever enough to get away with murder.

He started thinking what his punishment would be if pinned to the possum crimes. All he really did was relocate a few dead possums to some unusual places. The kidnapping however, might be a problem he thought to himself. He understood impersonating a police officer was a crime, but is impersonating a pizza guy such a big deal? These questions tumbled around in his head as he finished his sucker. He rolled down the window to throw the stick out and as he did he heard a scream in the distance, coming from his house.

With great urgency he gets out of the truck and runs full speed back towards home. His mind races even faster, wondering why did she scream? Did he leave any evidence around the house that Margret could find? She wouldn't go in his room right? Maybe there's a problem with Cody and Kyle. As fast as he ran his mind was working just as hard to come up with a scenario that didn't involve her finding out anything about his dark secret. As his mind searched the deepest corridors of his memories recalling every detail of the last few days, he thought of the worst case scenario. The books he left on the end table.

He emerged from the tree line and into his backyard, stopping for a moment to catch his breath, but returning to a full sprint when he notices the back door is wide open. Full speed ahead, he runs through the door just in time to see Margret hanging up the corded phone. The sight of Gary causes her to cry uncontrollably and she grabs a dirty knife from the pile of dishes in the sink.

"Stay away from me!" She screams, pointing the knife at Gary.

He grabs a dirty plate from the sink and holds it in front of him with both hands like a shield and takes a slow step forward.

"What's wrong?" He asks, sweating bullets. A chunk of caviar detaches from the plate and falls onto the floor.

Cody and Kyle stand behind the kitchen wall with their heads peering through the opening to the drama unfolding. Margret spins around and hustles over to the end table and picks up Sally's diary. Gary slowly follows her into the living room with his plate held high. She throws the diary at Gary as hard as she can and Gary thrusts the plate in forward motion knocking the book away.

"You're sick! I've seen your nasty projects in your shed, the newspaper clippings, the hat you stole from the poor pizza man!" She yelled, returning the knife up to a defensive position. "The police are on their way!" She said sobbing.

In a rage Gary wound up and twisted his whole body and threw the plate like a frisbee into the TV. The plate and screen shatter with a light show of sparks and glass. After the loud shattering sound the room got quiet. Gary looks down towards Cody and Kyle and his anger subsides. He gives them a nod.

"Yall are good kids, but I don't deserve friends."

And he turns around and backtracks through the kitchen and out the door, sprinting for the trees. Once he is out of sight of the house he leans up against a tree to try and settle his nerves. A deep breath is followed by an emotional breakdown. His knees buckle and his hands mute his wailing cries. He wipes his red eyes on his sleeve and gets back up and goes a little deeper into the woods. He walks past the red truck and then turns back around to grab some pizza from inside. He figured if he was going to live the outlaw life he would probably get hungry. With two slices of pizza, one in each hand, he strolls through the woods sniffling and munching down on his greasy dinner.

There was no coming back from this, there was no fixing any of it. He was done. He had to stay hidden, he thought to himself. He pondered where he could go or how to get anywhere but here. Maybe he could hide in a tree for a few days, then try escaping. Maybe he could find a stream or river and follow it to the ocean, then sail to a far away beach. His imagination was at work as he walked and ate and sniffled. His plotting is interrupted by movement up ahead of him. He could see a large creature's silhouette shuffling behind some brush. He took a bite of pizza and decided it wasn't worth his attention. He had to keep going so he altered his path to walk around the animal. The shape seemed to match Gary's trajectory and move to the side as he did. Gary stopped and so did the shape.

It was starting to get dark and he squinted his eyes to try and see better. He unholstered his pistol just to be safe and kept walking trying to maneuver around whatever this thing was. As he continued on, the sound of leaves and twigs rustling and snapping seemed to get louder as the shape started to position itself back in front of him. He stops and stares down the faint object with his pistol pointed in its direction as the large creature takes slow, almost methodical steps towards Gary. The moonlight has begun replacing the dusky rays. And as the thing draws closer, the dull light reflects off its antlers. Upon seeing this Gary seizes up, remembering the last time he encountered a deer in these woods. His sweaty palms and fingers fidget with the pistol as the deer moves. This deer looks much different than the charred embery beast from before. The deer looks like it has a sideways bend in its back as if it were broken. The almost L shaped torso created an eerie crab like rhythm in its walk as its disfigured body and legs crept closer. Coagulated black blood gathered around its eyes and mouth. A large open wound could be seen on its side, revealing muscle and tissue on the inside bend of the broken deer.

It stopped several feet away, its head cocked to the side not making eye contact. But Gary got the impression it did in fact see and notice him. He lowered his gun in amazement that this deer was alive and walking. Intrigued, he stared and examined it. And it just stood there with its head tilted, possibly looking back at him, but Gary was unsure. Starting to feel sorry for the creature he held out the crust from one of the pizzas. A part of him was hoping it would decline the offering and scurry away, but as he held out the food, the deer and its mangled body walked closer in the most unsettling fashion. The closer it got the urge to run increased, but he resisted and held his ground, crust extended. The deer drew close enough that Gary could hear its wheezing like breathing. It sniffs the crust before gently taking it out of Gary's hand. Gary let out a quick surprised chuckle, thrilled that this monster doesn't seem violent.

As the deer chews on the crust, Gary pets him gently on the head. The deer doesn't seem to mind as it continues to chow down on the salty treat. Once the deer finishes the treat, it stands as still as a statue. Gary waits to see what the animal will do next but it doesn't move a muscle. It doesn't even look like it is breathing anymore, it almost looks frozen in time. Uncomfortable and feeling uneasy, Gary takes a step to move around the deer. As he does, the animal lets out a sudden force of air through his nostrils and cocks his head rapidly to face Gary. His blood soaked eyes now locking with Gary's. He starts sniffing again, swaying his head back and forth close to Gary, who has to dodge the antlers from smacking him in the head. The deer zeroes in on his front shirt pocket and gives Gary's chest a nudge with its bloody black nose.

"Ok alright buddy hold on." He said to the deer as he reached in his pocket to grab a lollipop. At seeing the treat in his hand the deer again became stone still as Gary unwrapped the sucker. With caution he held out the bright red lollipop and the deer leaned in and popped it in its mouth. The stem rotated around and up and down as the deer enjoyed his sweet treat. Gary reaches up to pet the deer again but hears voices behind him. He turns his head around and sees beams of light spread throughout the woods dancing back and forth. One of the beams shines directly on his face.

"There! Over there!" An officer shouted.

Gary turns back around and sees the deer already in a full sprint, which for this animal looks very unnatural. Gary follows the deer deeper into the woods sprinting at full speed trying to catch up. His heart races, he runs and runs following the deers lead as it weaves in and out of the trees dodging branches. The moonlight pierces through the dark just enough for Gary to see the possum cages up ahead. The deer continues full speed towards the brush at the base of the hillside. As the deer gets within several feet of the bushes, a crackling moaning sound emits from the wild thick brush as it parts a path for the deer to go through. Too afraid to contemplate what he just witnessed he keeps following the deers path and runs into the opening in the brush. Branches and leaves whip him across his whole body as he runs through this dark tunnel of brush. He looks back behind him and just sees blackness at the center of this tunnel stretching out farther than he thought he had run. Looking back ahead he sees a faint light, he chases after it. The light grows bigger until it engulfs Gary and then vanishes.

Chapter **10**

Out of breath Gary collapses to his knees gasping for air. He looks around, trying to gather his bearings. The moon looks almost three times bigger than he remembers, bringing forth much more light than just moments ago on the other side of the strange tunnel. The trees look different than the ones from his backyard. These trees are taller and have a thicker trunk and they appear much older. The moonlight is more dense and dull. The light hitting the leaves of the trees give off a matte finish on the leaves. A thin soft blanket of translucent crimson fog sweeps across the forest floor. It's quiet apart from his heavy breathing. He turns one ear towards the tunnel trying to listen for the others who were after him, but eerie silence is all there is. He notices a white little stick on the top of the soil. He holds it close to his face and he sees some red near one end of it; the lollipop from the deer. After his breathing returns to normal, he stands up and brushes himself off. A twig snaps in the direction of the tunnel. Gary snaps around and draws his firearm. He waits without moving a muscle. Not seeing or hearing anymore disturbances he holsters the pistol and runs his hands through his hair.

"Where am I?" He mutters to himself.

He tries walking around to the side of the bushes he came out of in order to scope out the landscape. The brush is too tall and thick to see over and it spreads for miles in each direction. He thinks about the fact that from the perspective of his property, there was only a hillbank with bushes, so he should have had to travel uphill through the bushes but he never did, it's as if he went straight through the hill. This perplexed him greatly. He searched for any trees that he could possibly climb to get a better vantage point, but the lowest branches were too high up for him to climb.

With his adrenaline levels going down he begins to hear the sounds of the forest; buzzing and insects chirping in the distance. He is able to hear the subtle rustling of the leaves high above. He keeps listening and picks up the sound of running water. Parched and in need of hydration he decides to follow the sound of the water, his steps cut through the fog and the crimson clouds have a subtle pull towards his legs, as if it is drawn to him.

He makes his way through the forest, looking at all the unfamiliar plants that were never in his own backyard. Dark green ferns with black stems made up most of the vegetation. A three petaled gray flower littered the landscape filling in the spaces between the ferns. As he continued towards the sound of running water he came across a fallen tree. The trunk of the tree on the ground came up to his shoulders. Deep purple mushrooms with back rings circling the cap and red gills shot up from the moss in all directions of the log.

The sound of the water was getting louder. He knew he was getting close and picked up his pace. The brush gets thicker as he travels and he has to use both hands to try and clear a path. He moves a large fern leaf to the side and sees a river. He steps down a small ledge on some rocks and pebbles and walks to the water.

Gary sees the river and rubs his eyes.

"This is a dream, wake up idiot." He tells himself, slapping the sides of his cheeks with both hands. He walks right next to the water line trying to explain what is before him. The river stretches about fifty feet wide with some light rapids. The current of the river is unusual, in that it is flowing in two directions. The half closest to Gary is flowing to his left, the other half nearest the opposite bank flows to the right. Gary also noticed the crimson fog faded away over the other half of the river, and looking out at the opposite bank, there was no fog at all. The water looked dark, as if absorbing the moonlight to keep it hidden. Even though he was thirsty, he did not trust drinking out of this river.

He continues on and walks along the bank in the same direction as the current on the side of the bank he is on, the little rapids fade to a calm quiet flow. Unsure of what to do he wanders up the bank hoping to find food he can eat and water he can trust. Hours pass with nothing new in the scenery so he decides to head more inland hoping to have better luck. He continues fighting with the thick leaves and sticks as he clears a path through the woods. Another hour passes and the forest begins to thin. The trees are still massive but there are less of them. The density of the ferns and flowers lessens as he pursues through the forest. The journey has become much easier, not having to continually whisk away encroaching plants.

In need of a rest Gary sits down and leans against a tree and starts sucking on his last lollipop. He closes his eyes and falls asleep.

"Pssssst!"

Gary wakes up with a hand on his shoulder shaking him, his lollipop falling onto the ground. With a quick burst of speed Gary slaps the figure in front of him right in the face.

"OWWWWW!" The Figure yelled, flailing to the ground.

"Gah what the…." He says looking down at Kyle holding his face trying to stand back up.

Gary leaps to his feet, grabbing his lollipop on the way up. "What are you doing here?" He asks in a harsh whisper.

"I followed you, but you ran too fast after you gave the deer a lollipop and the cops were behind us."

"Wait you saw that? Why didn't you show yourself or something then?" he asked, surprised that Kyle was able to follow him this whole time without being seen.

"Well I didn't want to scare it away and when you started running after it I could barely keep up. I was too tired to run once I got in the tunnel."

"How did you find me here if you fell so far behind?" He asked.

"Well I saw you head into the woods so I ran to try and catch up but I couldn't find you. I could barely see anything. But I found a river and followed that for a while and then I heard something moving around in the woods and then I found you." He said with a smile.

"You got lucky you went left at the river. Who knows where you would be otherwise." Gary said, stretching his arms and back.

"I didn't go left, I went right." He replied.

Gary stopped dusting off his lollipop. "What?"

"At the river, I went to the right, upstream." he said slowly, making sure Gary heard him.

Gary bent down to meet Kyle's eye level. "Slap me as hard as you can in the face."

Kyle looked confused, but did what he said and wound up with his whole body and whipped his open palm right into the side of Gary's head.

A loud slapping sound pierced the quiet, half of his face bright red.

"Son of a…." Gary said, holding his face.

"Why did you tell me to do that?" Kyle asked.

"To see if I'm dead." He said, standing back up still rubbing his head.

"I guess we should keep moving, but we should also be quiet so let's keep the talking down. We have no idea what could be out here." Gary said in a concerned whisper. Kyle nodded his head in agreement. Gary unsheathed his knife from his ankle holster and handed it to Kyle.

Kyle took the knife and looked at Gary. Gary just gave him a nod and they ventured on.

They walked and weaved through the woods choosing their path with the least resistance. Kyle started to fall farther and farther behind as the night went on, growing more fatigued with every step. Gary waited for Kyle to catch up, pausing to look up and see the stars. To his surprise there weren't any. It was black, the only visible object was the oversized moon shining its light below. Kyle caught up and they kept wandering through the woods until Gary stopped dead in his tracks and swiftly raised a fist. Kyle mimicked Gary and froze behind him. Kyle began to ask Gary a question but Gary looked down at him fiercely with a finger drawn to his lips. Tapping his ear he pointed up ahead. Kyle nodded and listened. They heard movement up ahead, the crackling of leaves and debris as something moved as well as some snickering sounds coming from what sounded like multiple animals or creatures.

Gary led the way forward, tip-toeing up to a tree for cover, Kyle followed and they each peered around the tree. A large clearing was before them, there were only a few ferns and flowers up ahead, the ground was mostly dirt, leaves, and forest debris inhabiting this space, and there were many possums. They stared in amazement at the sight they were beholding, for it wasn't just any ordinary possums, but they had built a camp, they were organized.

There were cube-like hanging stations made of wood poles lashed together with twine. Dangling from the four sides of the lashed structure were skinned racoons. There were also two cross beams lashed across the top of the cube and more dangling racoons, swaying in the light of the nearby fire. Their heads were lopped off and sat in a pile off to the side next to another pile of their gray and black striped pelts. One possum was peeling the skin off the last racoon with skin and a head. The possum was on two feet using a pocket knife cutting and peeling the fur off. Once the skin was off he put the knife down and grabbed a multi tool off of a little wood slab that acted as a table. The saw blade of the multi tool was already folded out and ready to use, and the possum started sawing off the head of the skinless racoon. The head came off quickly, it seemed this creature was very experienced at his work. He then separated the skin and the head in the two piles.

The possum was feeding multiple fires with racoon heads and sticks. He would pull a bundle of branches from a crudely built shed next to his decapitation station and throw them into the rock enclosed fire pits. Next he tossed a couple of racoon heads in the flames and placed metal grates over the fires that rested on some taller stones. The possum swapped the saw for the knife and started slicing away cuts of meat from a racoon and threw them on the grates, preparing a feast for the table of possums next to the cook station.

A very large fallen branch was carved into an unevenly rectangular table that sat about twenty possums on each side. They were sitting on circular wooden stools cut from the stumps of smaller trees. The table was set with actual plates, and while they waited for the food to be ready they drank from a variety of cups. Coffee cups with broken handles, a small thermos, and some plastic sippy cups made up most of the glassware of this dinner party.

At the front of the table a few feet back, a larger tree stump carved into an elaborate throne looked over the table. The throne has wooden steps carved into the base of it. The sides of the arm rest had intricate carvings of trees and flowers. On top of this throne sat a large overweight possum, the largest one of this group. Many scars covered the gray and white fur of the possum. A crown of sticks and leaves wrapped around its head. He wore a cloak made of racoon fur, with rusty iron clasps and a chain keeping it on. The racoon tail of the cloak wrapped around the sitting king and dangled next to his feet. His beady eyes were a solid flat crimson red color. He just sat there with his hands on his belly looking bored waiting for the food to be ready.

On the ground level standing upright on each side of the possum king are two bright white possums. Each possum wore a cloak similar to the king, but they were hooded and made of skunk pelts. The arms of the skunk pelts wrapped around their shoulders and connected across the chest with a simple gold clasp. The tails of the skunk cloak were cut short so as not to drag in the dirt. The white possums eyes were a solid pale blue.

What really baffled Gary and Kyle the most was what was on the other side of the table, directly in the king's view as if placed there as decoration or a trophy to behold. At the end of the table opposite of the king were cages. Two cages built of thick sticks and ropes. Each cage was roughly four feet tall in the shape of a cube. A chain wrapping around and locking each of the cage doors. The people inside were bound by ropes around their mouths, hands, and feet. They sat up leaning up against the back of the cage facing the table of possums and the king.

"Are those people in there?" Kyle whispered to Gary, his lips quivering.

"Ya, I'm pretty sure those are people, let's get a better look." He said darting to the next tree.

Scared, Kyle followed close behind, holding on to the back of Gary's shirt. Gary slapped his hand away in annoyance. A handful of possums heard the slap and turned around towards them. They hugged the tree and peered one eye back out to see if they were still looking. The king pointed to a possum at the table and then pointed in the direction of the boys behind the tree. One possum marched towards them, and they fully retreated behind the tree.

"You better be ready with that knife." Gary said sternly to the kid.

"Me?" Kyle whispered back in defiance.

"No your brother Cody, yes you, I can't shoot the thing because then our cover will really be blown. If he comes around the tree and sees us, just stab it in the neck or something. It's not that hard. Possum's are squishy. Only if that thing sees us. Got it?"

Kyle leans his back against the tree bark and slides down to the ground. With both hands he clutches the knife and waits. The tiny footsteps get louder as the possum gets closer. Kyle's knuckles turn white gripping the knife. Then, the possum stops and puts out its hand to lean against the tree right next to Kyle. Kyle holds his breath, his eyes as wide as the dinner plates the possums are about to eat off of. The possum wrinkles its nose and sniffs around, then starts walking past him. He zigs and zags on his two feet, then tumbles into some leaves. The possum falls down on four legs and stumbles drunkenly past Kyle back to the table.

Gary gives a thumbs up, then motions Kyle to stand up. They crouch down and sneak to a fallen tree with more of the blue and black mushrooms growing out from it. Covertly they make their way to the end of the log bringing them plenty close to get a better view of the cages. Gary peeks over the top, Kyle being too short has to look around the side of the log. They see the two people tied up in the cages more clearly. One of the cages sits a man in his thirties, matted dirty brown hair with a face full of stubble. His clothes were all torn up and falling apart. They looked very old. He wore blue jeans and a short sleeve button down. Scars covered his arms and neck and some on his face. They were small and jagged like a bunch of tiny bite marks.

The other cage had a young woman locked inside. She was very dirty and had wild long wavy hair. She had striking blue eyes and was also wearing jeans, but with a t-shirt. Her clothes were also worn and tattered.

Gary turned pale as a ghost and the log caught his body as he nearly fainted collapsing forward. Kyle had a different reaction, filled with energy, delight, and fear, he shouts at the top of his lungs, "Dad!".

Every single possum turned its head.. The clanging of glassware and social chatter ceased. The king and the two guards glared at the intruders, the whole table of possums silent and still. With a crooked rodent finger the possum king called them out from their hiding place.

Gary steps out from hiding first, then waves at Kyle to join him by his side. With great intrigue the possum king examines the two newcomers. Gary and Kyle just stand in front of this possum audience unsure of what is going to happen next, just watching being watched. Kyle starts to fidget, his nerves getting the best of him, Gary gives him a look and a nod of assurance that everything is okay. The king strokes his long thin chin hair and raises a closed fist in the air. The creaking of wood from tightening bowstrings is heard from two archers nests in the trees behind the king. Before he could issue the fire command, Gary had already reacted by taking out his pistol and firing at the archers. With three rapid shots he takes out the archers on the left. The first possum he hit in the head, blood sprays up and against the tree as it falls limp in the nest. The other two were hit directly in the chest, and they tumbled out of the nest falling into the ferns below.

The other three archers in the adjacent nest fire at will. Two tiny arrows sink into Gary's shoulder and leg, and one pegs Kyle in the knee. If they were full sized arrows being shot by humans, much more damage would have been dealt. Blood trickled from where they were hit. Kyle yells out in pain holding his stinging knee. Gary grips his firearm with both hands and with a swift sweeping motion fires on all three. Each of the three possums take a bullet to the head. One after another their heads explode into bloody glory. The possums at the table scurry away, retreating on all fours into the woods. Gary checks the ammo count in the clip of his smoking gun.

Seconds later all the possums that scurried away came running back running on two legs, holding kitchen knives, meat tenderizers, hammers and all kinds of melee weaponry. In an organized formation they surround the throne in an attack ready position. With both hands the king points to the two white robed possums on his left and right, and directs them forward like a flight attendant giving a safety demonstration. They barge through to the very front of the formation. The one on the left looks at the other and nods, then bends over and scoops up a handful of dirt and crimson fog. Like a connoisseur of fine wine he swirls the dirt and fog in his hand until it starts sparking. The swirling intensifies until a full flame rests in his tiny possum palm, and with a quick flick of the wrist a solid beam of white hot fire hurls towards Gary and Kyle.

Gary grabs Kyle and dives behind the log. The ray of fire collides with the bark of the fallen tree and within seconds it blasts through the thick truck out the other side a few feet above their heads as they lay in the dirt trying to stay as low as they can. Gary sits up once the fire subsides and aims through the new opening in the log, locks on to the fire casting possum, and pulls the trigger.

The white possum sees Gary return to a firing position through the glowing orange hole in the fallen log, embers smoking from the blast. It bends down and takes two handfuls of the crimson fog and flings it up in the air into a protective barrier. The bullet wisps into the fog and disappears. The king lets out a yowling hissing battle cry and the army of possums charge forward.

Shots ring out of the pistol, dropping possums to the ground only to be trampled by their charging brethren. He ejects the empty clip and loads in the next one. He continues to fire upon the charging army, blood splatters with each well aimed shot as possums tumble to their demise. Heads continue to explode and little fury chests are blasted wide open. By the time he empties the clip, the creatures have reached the other side of the log and are clawing their way over the top.

"Get ready." Gary says to Kyle.

Kyle, not sure what to do, holds the knife up out above his head with both hands. Gary loads his last spare magazine into his pistol. The creatures start to appear over the top of the log meeting Gary's eye level. Gary returns to shooting but the swarm overruns the log. With a loud hiss a possum leaps from the top of the log with a rusty hammer towards Kyle. The knife penetrates through the torso of the possum and slides down the blade to Kyle's hand. Kyle lets out a high pitched squeal that is soon drowned out by a possum leaping from the log and landing on his face. The possum hisses and starts pulling out Kyle's hair and scratching his head. Gary, hearing the muzzled screams of the child, takes careful aim and blasts the possum right open through the side of its torso. Rodent blood mists all over Kyls face mixing with his own blood now dripping from the scratches on his head.

Kyle turns to run away but trips on a rock, the arrow in his knee snaps off leaving just the arrowhead. He cries out in pain and rolls on his back just in time to see a critter scurrying over with a hatchet swinging in its paws. Kyle takes the knife and stabs it into the neck of the possum, it goes limp on the blade, the little hatchet falling in the dirt.

Gary now backs up as he fires, trying to be conscious of his targets, not wanting to waste ammo. He makes his way towards Kyle who is madly slicing oncoming possums left and right as he lay on the ground. Streaks of blood wick off the blade and into the air with each swing. All of the possums made it over the log like a swarm of ants and scurry around taking swings with their various weaponry. One possum raises a pizza cutter attempting to slice Gary's shin but he dodges the swing, then punts the creature like a football and shoots it mid air. At that moment Gary feels something sharp sting his buttocks, then rip back out tearing his pants and his flesh. He faces his aggressor to see a snarling beast swinging a casual dress belt with nails sticking out of it. It takes another swing, Gary breaks off a thick branch from the log and deflects the blow. The belt wraps around the stick and Gary rips it out of the possum's paw. Now wielding a club with a spiked belt wrapped around it, he smashes the animal over and over until nothing is left but a pile of organs and red meat.

Kyle still fighting with his back on the ground tallies up quite a death count with bloody possums piling up around him. Swinging and stabbing at anything that moves. Beating a few more possums with the club, Gary moves back and helps clear the last few possums on top of Kyle. He golf swings a large possum with a big gut with his spiked club. The possum's stomach shreds open as it flies into the air leaving a trail of intestines. A possum nipping at Kyle's ears sees Gary and lunges at him. His claws dig into his shirt and pierce his skin hissing and gnawing violently at his chest. He drops the club and grabs the possum with both hands prying it off of his flesh, chunks of skin and red flesh dangle in the claws of the possum. Enraged by this creature, Gary twists the possum like he is wringing out a wet towel. The possum lets out an excruciating death cry as its back breaks and its muscles pop and twist. With all his strength while standing over Kyle, Gary lets out a battle cry and rips the possum in half. The blood sprays out and trickles all over Kyle's torso and soaks into his shirt. Two possums flank from each side. Simultaneously they run and jump at Gary. Still holding the two pieces of the torn in half creature, he punches one of the possums directly in the head, the impact was strong enough to instantly snap its neck. The other one latches on to his leg directly under his holster. Gary lifts the gun up just enough to pull the trigger and sends a bullet through the holster and into the possum.

More possums file in and try to take advantage of Kyle still being knocked prone. They swarm to each side running over the many dead corpses already around Kyle. Gary faces the oncoming possums to Kyle's left side as Kyle flails his knife around swinging and cutting up more possums on the other side. The first wave tries to run past Gary to get to Kyle. The attempt fails when Gary lifts his boot and smashes the leader. The others in the wave turn their focus on Gary and try to charge up his leg. One of the possums climbs up and stabs him in the thigh with a pair of rusty scissors. Gary yells and grabs the scissors out of the possum's hands and cuts its head off with one swift cut of the scissors. The remaining possums are on his leg. He has to rip them off with his bare hands and throw them as far as he can. When they come back one by one Gary is able to finish them off with the club and his boots.

The dead mound of possums covering Kyle has become so large it is at the point where the possum's only way to attack is through an opening in the center of the mound on top. The critters run up and into the possum volcano only to be met by an eruption of jabs from Kyle's bloody blade. The last possum falls victim to the knife and fills the hole of the mound, covering Kyle completely in bloody rodent carcassess.

Eventually five possums make a semi circle around Gary and Kyle. The ground thick with blood soaks into their fur. Kyle emerges to his feet, bloody corpses rolling off of him like a child emerging from a pile of leaves. His clothes are dark red and heavy. The five remaining creatures look around at all of their slaughtered brethren, then at each other, and then drop their weapons and retreat into the woods.

"You alright?" Gary asked, as he felt his ripped pants from the back.

Kyle is traumatized, covered in blood from his head to his toes, and says nothing back. Gary peers through the opening in the log and sees the two white possums and the king. He checks his ammo. He has a few bullets left. He clicks the clip back in and holsters his gun and walks around the log with his hands up. Kyle, too traumatized to know what to do, follows him around to the clearing, hobbling like a zombie. Upon seeing them present themselves victorious in the battle, the possum king steps down from his throne.

"Drop the knife kid." Gary says.

Kyle snaps out of his daze. " What, why?" He asks.

"They burnt a freaking hole in a five foot thick log using dirt clods. You ain't gonna do jack all with that thing."

Kyle gently places the knife in the dirt. He picks up a handful of soil and fog and stands back up. He starts swirling it in his hand, then throws it as hard as he can towards the king and guards. Nothing happens. One of the white possums snickers and picks a stone up off the ground. The fog wicks off of it like water as he raises it up and levitates it above his palm. With a quick flick he faces his palm towards Kyle and the rock spirals like a rocket and slams into the knee without the arrow stuck in it. He howls in pain and collapses back to the ground.

Gary's eyes follow the stone as it drops his friend. He lowers his hands slowly, looking down toward the screaming child. He waits a bit, thinking of what to do. Trying not to telegraph his next move, without looking he draws his pistol and shoots a shot from the hip. The white possum has no time to react and the bullet makes contact with its arm blowing it clean off. Gary then turns and continues firing at the king and guards. The possums scurry on all fours dodging the projectiles. Each possum grabs onto some fog and pulls it over them like a blanket, rolling around on the ground until they vanish from sight.

Gary drops his gun and falls to his knees and lets out a sigh of relief. Kyle crawls over to him and tugs on his shirt. Gary looks down and sees Kyle handing him the knife.

"I don't want it anymore." He said sniffling.

"Tough." Gary said.

In the heat of the battle they had forgotten about the cages until they heard the muffled screams of Charlotte and Kyle's dad. With urgency they ran toward the cages to help them out.

"How do we get them out without the key?" Kyle said, pulling on the padlock.

Gary rolled his eyes and yanked the knife out of his hand and started cutting away at the ropes that lashed the wooden bars together. The wall to the first cage fell down and Kyle rushed in to untie his dad. Gary ran over to Charlotte and cut down the cage wall and unbound her. They embraced each other with tears of joy, not letting go for a long time.

"You don't look a day older than when I last saw you. How is that possible?" Gary asked, looking down at her baby bump, teary eyed and sniffling. Charlotte had no answer and pulled Gary close and hugged him some more.

Kyle untied his dad and embraced him.

"Are you Cody or Kyle?" The dad asked on the brink of crying.

"Kyle." He said, weeping into his chest.

Holding his son for the first time he broke down in uncontrollable tears of relief and happiness.

Once the tears subsided, they helped each other off their feet. Gary put his hands on his wife's shoulder.

"I'm going to get you out of here." He said.

She responded with a subtle smile with hope in her watery eyes.

"She can't leave this place." A booming voice said from the forest.

Bushes crack and break and tree branches snap as they are moved out of the way by a full size panda bear stepping into the clearing. It wore a brown sun kissed leather messenger bag around its chest and accompanied by a small critter wearing a cloak on its shoulder. Gary goes to draw his pistol but his hands grasp at air. He looks over and finds it in the dirt.

"Relax, you're probably out of ammo anyway. We did hear a lot of commotion after all." He said and let out a bellowing chuckle.

"Don't you lay a finger on Charlotte!" Gary yelled in a frenzy pointing a finger towards the panda. "We are getting out of here and if you stand in our way you will end up like your little friends." He pointed to the battlefield of corpses.

"You don't understand." The bear said empathetically. "You said it yourself, she doesn't look a day older than when you last saw her, right? When was the last time you saw her?"

He looks at Charlotte in disbelief that she looks so young and beautiful just like he remembers.

"About ten years ago." He said sorrowfully.

"Well then, I take it she has been raised by the fog, and now she cannot live without it. The dead don't lie for long in these parts." He explained. Kyle and Gary now look quite confused.

"What is he talking about?" Gary asks Charlotte.

"There is something wrong with this place Gary. I don't understand it but I have seen countless things here that I can't explain." She says with a strained voice.

Gary turns back to the panda, his face begging for an explanation.

"Look." The bear said, "You can't get her out, at least not by yourself. But we can help."

"Who even are you?" Gary said exasperated at the lack of information.

"My apologies for the lack of introduction." He points to the critter on his shoulder. "This is Gilby, a descendant of Ludgrig, the most powerful mage I've had the pleasure of knowing: breaking away from the path of his bloodline to pursue a higher calling."

The hooded figure pulls back his black hood. His beady rat eyes shone a shimmering green in the moonlight. He had brown fur and chubby cheeks with long white droopy whiskers. Gilby bowed respectfully and put his hood back on. Gary and Kyle looked even more confused at what the panda was talking about. Charlotte and Kyle's dad were unphased by the quirky duo; they have seen plenty of wild things in this realm.

"We find willing wanderers and help them escape these cursed parts. Which leads me to…" He looks at his feet to his left, then right, then turns all the way around and speaks into the woods. "Don't be shy friends."

An undersized possum and a racoon appear from the brush and sit next to the panda's feet.

"This is Randel." He points to the possum on his left. The possum tucks his head into the panda's fur.

"And this is Joyce." He points to the raccoon on the right, she bows and gracefully lifts a paw.

"These are the wanderers we have found thus far on our journey eager to flee these cursed lands. You are welcome to join us if you like. Your chances on your own are, well, impossible." He said rummaging through his leather bag.

"What is this curse you keep talking about?" Gary asks impatiently.

"I was killed, Gary." Charlotte speaks up.

"What? That's impossible." He said, grabbing her hand.

"Like I said Gary, the fog has raised her, and him as well." The panda says gesturing towards Kyle's dad.

"All of these creatures you see lying before you will soon be raised by the fog. There is no escaping it. As long as your members are intact, the fog will take you." He looked at the hanging rack of the headless and skinned racoons. "Them, probably not so much, but this battlefield will not be sleeping for long. We must go before they wake."

"Who are you? You never gave a name." Gary asked, less irritated and beginning to understand the severity of the situation.

"Ah, forgive me again. Introductions are not in my wheelhouse of skills I suppose. I am Crumbauzer, but my closest friends and family simply call me Crumb.